A Part of Me

Is

Missing

A Part of Me Is Missing

by

Alexander M. Ross

Alexander M. Ross

Borealis Press Ltd.
Ottawa, Canada
2002

Corrections pp. 23, 96
by the author

Canadä

The Publishers acknowledge the financial assistance of the
Government of Canada through the Book Publishing
Program (BPIDP) for our publishing activities.

National Library of Canada Cataloguing in Publication Data

Ross, Alexander M., 1916-
    A part of me is missing

ISBN 0-88887-197-X

    1. Title.

PS8585.O834P37 2002   C813'.6   C2001-903878-X

The characters in this work are fictional; any resemblance to
actual persons, living or dead, is purely coincidental.

Cover: design by Bull's Eye Design, Ottawa, Canada.

Printed and bound in Canada on acid free paper

Dedication

Do Alasdair, m'ogha gaolach

"The web of our life is of a mingled yarn, good and
ill together."

Shakespeare
All's Well That Ends Well, IV.iii

Other Publications of Alexander M. Ross

William Henry Bartlett, Artist, Author, Traveller. University of Toronto Press, 1973.

The College on the Hill, a History of the Ontario Agricultural College, 1874-1974. Copp Clark, 1974.

The Imprint of the Picturesque on Nineteenth-Century British Fiction. Wilfrid Laurier University Press, 1986.

Slow March to a Regiment. Vanwell Publishing, 1993.

A Year and a Day. Essence Publishing, 1997.

Joint Author

Alexander M. Ross and Terry Crowley. *The College on the Hill, a New History of the Ontario Agricultural College 1874-1999*: Dundurn Press, 1999.

Contents

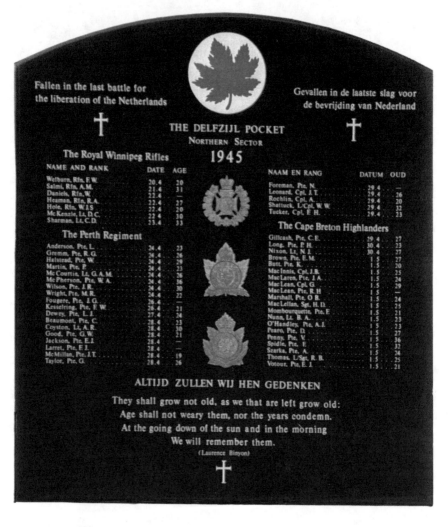

The memorial plaque in the Holwierde church

Holwierde, Netherlands
"the pretty village of Holwierde," p. 84

Holwierde, Netherlands, after 24 April, 1945

Chapter 1

Christie Street

Towards the end of her night shift, Sister Fleda always slipped in on us silently while we were still half asleep. Tactically the advantage was hers for she could get on with her work without having to hear questions or complaints or endure our witticisms. Impossible of course to talk or even reply to her cheerful, "How are you this morning?" with a thermometer under your tongue as she was counting your pulse beat.

That over with me, her inspection became a bit embarrassing: "Now let's have a peek at your bottom." With me flat on my stomach, she'd remove the covers, slide the hospital gown to my shoulders, and jerk one of the adhesive strips loose to look inside the dressing. "Healing nicely and clean," she'd pronounce as she replaced the adhesive. "Now let's see the end of your leg." That inspection approved of, there followed a chilling alcohol rub, the re-arranging of my gown and covers, and her parting quip: "You'll be off with the Perths any day now—just you wait."

By the time she'd made the rounds of the patients in our end of the ward, which was divided a third of the way down by a nursing station, we were all awake. Some of us in my end were looking after our needs in the lavatory while orderlies were tending to bed patients. Altogether nearly thirty beds lined the wall of the ward. Impossible to know everyone.

We were in my end of the room a mixed lot nearly all infantry—save for a lone gunner. Two of the men not far from my bed bore my name, McKay, but spelling it MacKay. The nearest, who had lost both his legs above the knee, even had my Christian name, James. He had a radio which was treasured by all of us near enough to hear the programmes and newscasts. The other MacKay, four beds farther on, was blind; he had a false nose and no arms below the elbows—and interestingly my father's name, John. Just beyond him was the gunner, a man from Saskatchewan on whom we lavished much false sympathy:

"It's just too damned bad you have to be here, gunner. After all you were only two miles behind our battalion headquarters, and we thought we'd cleared all the Jerries out of that area. Sure you weren't a bit careless, old chap?"

Most of us were easily identified, but the MacKays and I were often mistaken by nurses and orderlies. Earlier, when I first arrived at Christie Street, Sister Fleda had asked me to which lot of McKays I belonged.

"Oh, we're the McKay Blacks," I told her, "from the 3rd Concession of West Zorra."

"And what's your nearest town?"

"Embro, but it's really only a village."

"And so," she went on, "you're one of the McKay Blacks. That's interesting." Pausing, while adjusting her chart, she asked, "But why Blacks?"

"Because my father's people were dark skinned and had black hair and dark brown eyes."

"But your hair," she countered, "is fair and your eyes are as blue as mine. Why are you different?"

"I'm not sure although my aunt in Woodstock—my mother's sister—is a blonde. Mother's pictures show her as a brunette, she's white now."

"And what do the neighbours call you?"

"Just McKay Black's boy. Actually," I went on, "my

Old Man nearly always called me 'Boy'."

Anxious to get to other patients, Sister left me saying, "That settles it; from now on I shall call you Boy—I can keep track of two of your tribe, but three's just one too many."

And the name stayed. As MacKay No Legs told me, it suited me for I had, despite my scarred face, a boyish appearance. Although I'd been in the Christie Street Military Hospital since mid-June in 1945, it was not easy always to put names on the fifteen or sixteen patients on our end of the ward. Much coming and going took place. Some, more permanent than others, were easily identified, often because of their wounds. "Far Bed" I knew by his location and his desire to talk with or without a listener. Part way down I could name Tim McGuire from the Toronto Irish; he'd lost both his right leg and right arm in a motorcycle accident when his machine and a mortar bomb coincided at a road junction. It was not easy either to remember the names of all the nursing sisters or the orderlies whose identities tended to blur as they alternated between day and night routines and sometimes had duties in other wards of our sprawling red-brick building. Sister Fleda's distinctive bearing and sympathy for our misfortunes made her unmistakable.

She was, the ward admitted, a good sort accepting us as we were, attentive to our needs and complaints, jollying us when we were low but never dropping her professional mien as she swept from one bed to another. With us she was Sister, out of hearing range she was known as die Fleder, a sobriquet that McGuire, an admirer of Johann Strauss, had given her as he noted her quiet evening swoops into the ward whenever one of us was about to open a clandestine bottle of Crown Royal. It was not confiscated but issued out to us in tots so that neither we nor Christie Street's bedding was at any risk.

About her a kind of aerial propriety set any hope of dalliance adrift in the longing mind; it was a propriety that led some patients to hint darkly that it was a mask behind which lurked interesting possibilities. Far Bed would in her absence plaintively hypothesize his hope: "Geez, how I'd like to roll with her in the clover." Save for the gunner's muttered, "some roll you'd have," we ignored Far Bed's fantasy, even pitied him for we knew he had to sit down to pee. It was his bad luck to have his penis sheered off in a shell burst while crossing the Melfa River. Undaunted, he continually forgot his loss as he titillated us with his imagined sexual legerdemain.

As days in the ward ran their course, Sister Fleda's attentions impressed me. Quietly capable she was a person whose sympathy for us was never maudlin, more often felt than declared. Once, as she stood waiting for the reading in her thermometer, her fingers traced the course of the scar that wrinkled my face from the lower lip to my right ear—as ragged as it was deaf. She said nothing, but the next night as she came on duty, she brought a tube of cocoa cream which she rubbed into the rough scar advising me to do so myself each day until the skin softened. From then on she'd often, after recording my temperature and pulse, feel the scar and ask if I were remembering to apply the cream. Her attentions to me stirred "No Legs" to wit: "Oh please Sister do what you can about his face, it bothers me, it's out of focus."

Sensuously, her attention to my scar resonated much more emotionally than her treatment of my buttock or stump. As she leant smiling over me, I could look into her steady blue flecked eyes, see her fair hair greying in streaks tucked under her cap, and smell faintly the perfume or powder she'd used on her body. About her appearance and care there was a rare simplicity that appealed and of which, I'm sure, she was unaware.

To me at that time, she became plainly desirable—not sexually so much as a presence I wanted near me. And I was almost grateful for the scar that brought her so near —almost appreciative of the German sniper beyond the Riccio who had failed to kill me because in the early morning light his aim had been minutely off the bull's eye.

But this emotional absurdity often faced competing low spirits as I sought to forget a death I'd meted out to a young German in Ceprano or tried to imagine how I was ever going to make peace with my father. His last words to me in the kitchen after breakfast, when I told him I was unavailable for the haying because I'd enlisted, were scathing: "You dim-witted bastard." Mother's instant objection to such language in the house did bring a half-hearted apology: "Well maybe I've gone too far—but only a dimwit. . . ." His voice trailed off to a mumble as he grabbed his coat from the hook on the door and set off for the barn leaving me crestfallen and mother white-faced and in tears. It was the last time in four years that I saw either of them. But mother did write to me, when they had word of my being wounded the first time, and regularly from then on.

During those four years I often remembered the farm and how spitting mad the Old Man was when I left him alone in the midst of haying. Now I wondered how I could, scarred and missing a leg, find favour at home, especially with my father whose fields I had left so thoughtlessly for the uncertainties of those a wide ocean away. The question left me distressed, something that Sister Fleda often sensed.

"And why the long face, what's troubling you this evening?" I'd been curt in response to her cheerful inquiry as to how things had gone throughout the day. On telling her only that I was worried about my future, her response was immediate:

"Oh, come now Boy, let the future look after itself. It's right now that matters. You're getting about better than most patients on crutches, you'll have a new leg before long, and a holiday, too. I've just learned that you have permission to spend next weekend with your parents. So cheer up, Boy! Think of all your friends on this ward who can't go home. We're all missing something—if the truth were told—and nothing can now be done about it."

I could not counter Sister's criticism of my gloom, and I was unwilling to tell her of the rift with the Old Man. For the next few days I tried to appear cheerful as she made her rounds. Ward chatter, visiting groups, the CBC programmes and news helped divert my nagging worries as did the circulation of the daily issues of *The Globe and Mail* telling us of Canadian soldiers rioting in Aldershot, of the thousands of tons of bombs being dropped on Japanese cities, and of George Drew's clashes in the legislature with Mr. Jolliffe. For some Canadians the war was now over, for others of us it would inevitably lengthen out according to our mental and physical scars.

But the week did slowly pass while I thought constantly of the Old Man and how he'd react to a son on crutches. Early in the week I spoke to my mother on the telephone who was very excited to hear I could come home; she assured me that she and father would meet my train in Stratford. Father, she said, was as anxious to see me as she was. I was relieved.

Another worry now surfaced. What should I take them? Taking gifts to friends or relatives whom we had not seen for a long time was an observance my mother never neglected. It would be for me now something more than a convention if it could help restore my place in the family. (All of what I tell you now happened, of course, well before I ventured to put my waywardness into words that might serve as a sort of self-exorcism—an excuse, if you scorn religious repentance.)

But, at the time I write about, my concerns narrowed down to the sort of gifts that might best curry favour with the penates of the household on the 3rd Concession, something to serve as a palliative for my neglect. Against the past stood my parents on the family farm—a farm designed as my inheritance. How could I ever manage to meet the homegrown expectations they had cherished for their only child? Dodging for the time this self-made issue, I devoted all my attention to suitable gifts. Father's was the more easily chosen because I knew he always liked a good brier tobacco pipe. With little more trouble than a telephone call I got a Savinelli one for him. My mother's gift was a greater challenge, and I'd almost succumbed to a five-pound box of Laura Secord chocolates when I noticed a Brodey-Draimin advertisement in the paper for mink scarves at $45.00 a skin. On my telephoning the shop on Yonge Street, a clerk recommended two skins for a scarf. Furthermore, the clerk assured me, on my asking about fox which I'd seen on some of our visitors, that mink was just as fashionable and, he added, more distinguished, becoming a favourite with many city ladies. With this assurance, I asked that two skins as a scarf be sent to me at my Christie Street address. The day the skins arrived, I showed them to Sister Fleda who asked teasingly if they were for her.

"No, they're a present for my mother," I said. "Do you think she'll like them?"

"Oh, I'm sure she'll be pleased—any mother would be. You must like her a great deal to give her so lovely a present. Was she always kind to you?"

"Yes, she was—always," I replied. "I liked her better than my father whose good common sense always assorted better with his land and animals than it did with me or my mother."

"And what are you taking to him?"

"Just a classy brier pipe, something that contributes to his ease of mind at the end of a hard day's work."

"Well, you are a good boy, and you must tell me on your return how you managed at home and what your mother thought of this lovely scarf."

On Saturday morning with Sister Fleda's help I left the hospital, my gifts in a small bag tied to one of my crutches, my empty trouser leg pinned up, and took a cab to Union Station where sympathetic red caps and a conductor managed to get me on my train. There I relaxed thinking rather selfishly of how good it would be even for a weekend to be free of the ward and its constant reminders of the penalties imposed on young men for winning a war.

In a coach half filled I remembered the crowded troop trains both in Canada and in England where even elbow space in a corridor was welcome. I remembered, too, how often I'd taken the train to and from Guelph for four years in all seasons except summer. About an hour out of Toronto, I noticed how every hill and valley seemed fittingly where it should be. It was also reassuring to see no roofless, shell-pocked buildings and no emaciated Dutch or ragged Italian people standing forlornly at wayside stations. The conductor's call, "Stratford, the next stop, this way out please" abruptly ended my wartime musings.

Chapter 2

Back Home

The meeting in Stratford's CN Station was emotional, mother in tears, father's voice out of control and I— touched as well—trying to appear upright as I leaned on my crutches. Mother and father hovered over me anxiously as we moved off to the old Chevy, father carrying my haversack and mother trying without success to take the parcel off my crutch. Once I and my belongings were stowed in the back seat, we set out for home, the parents brushing aside indignantly my offer to take them to a restaurant for supper on the grounds that an oven dinner was awaiting my arrival at home.

Just west of Stratford we turned south to follow a route I knew even better than the rail one to and from Guelph. Nothing had changed on the 4th Concession: the rolling farm lands, the long valley down to Brooksdale, and the side road over to the 3rd Concession—all home territory where I could put family names to the farms we passed and on the 3rd even recognize an old acquaintance at work on his land.

Home, shortly after three, I was surprised, even relieved, to find it looked exactly the same as, when smarting from the Old Man's stinging rebuff, I'd left it four years before. The house was a rambling old frame one sheltered on the north side by tall spruce trees. From the shade of one of them, our dog Caesar limped out to meet me. He quickly decided that crutches made me an alien to be growled at while his tail's gyrations expressed his pleasure at seeing my parents.

The three kitchen steps safely mounted, I stood in a mist of delicious odours, the sort we'd all fantasized about Overseas. Once in the kitchen, mother seized an apron and swept into action while father gave me a hand to a chair. It was then I embarrassed mother. "Where," I whispered to father, "is the john?" Hearing my question, my mother's face dropped.

"Oh Jamie, we haven't one yet because we haven't got the hydro—you'll have to go to the Lilacs—I'm sorry."

Lilacs was a euphemism to cover the purpose of a building that the Old Man called the backhouse and which was reserved principally for women. Men used the gutters behind vacant stalls in the stables. Three months in well-equipped hospitals and I'd forgotten the plumbing arrangements at home that were, as I thought about them, a good deal more private than the latrines I'd used in barracks and battle. So it was back on my crutches, down the kitchen's three steps and out to the Lilacs, no longer in flower.

Dinner shortly after five in the dining room was memorable, a tribute to my mother's timing skills with the McClary's oven and warming closet. The Barred Rock cockerel that had lost its head, feathers, and innards the day before was moved from the roasting pan out to the platter: a plump, succulent feast surrounded by oven-browned potatoes and supported by dishes of new garden carrots and green peas. Mother as usual carved to eliminate any possibility of her husband spilling gravy on the snow-white tablecloth she'd laid for the occasion.

It was Geoffrey, the hired man, an Englishman, whom I'd never met, who opened the conversation by asking if I knew where Hailsham was in England.

"Just north of Eastbourne," I told him. "I spent a weekend there once when the Regiment was for a short time quartered about Eastbourne. Why do you ask?"

"My home was near there," Geoffrey said, and after a pause, "I'd like some day to see it and the Downs again." This said, Geoffrey fell silent as my father inquired why I had to be back in Toronto on Monday.

"I have to be there on Monday afternoon for a prosthetic measurement which was arranged for two weeks ago."

"And what's a prosthetic measurement? I've never heard of such a thing."

"It's what's necessary," I informed him, "before an artificial leg and foot can be designed. The leg part especially has to be shaped so that it fits comfortably over my stump. Once that's done and, if the boot part is right, I'll be able to walk about like the rest of you."

"And who pays for that?" he asked, always alive to the expense of anything that had to do with doctors and hospitals.

"The Army," I told him. "I'm looked after until I'm discharged from the hospital and even after that, I believe, because my disability is permanent."

Relieved the Old Man turned his attention to the dessert, a seductive chocolate layer cake iced and with an almond cream filling.

"No one," I said to mother, as I accepted a second slice, "can make a better chocolate cake than you do."

"Well thank you, Jamie; I don't get many compliments for my cooking. Are you sure you're not just saying that so I'll make another one for you when you come back?"

"Just telephone me when you're putting it in the oven, and I'll be on my way."

"Expect a call any day," she told me smiling. "But what are the meals like at your hospital? Do you get enough to eat?"

"Yes, I think we do, but there's nothing like your fresh vegetables or your roast chicken. Still I must admit the meals there are a sight better than army grub."

The taciturn Geoffrey, having also had a second piece of cake, now announced that it was time to get the cows for milking and taking up his straw hat he set off with Caesar at his heels. Shortly after, father, having changed into overalls and smock, moved off to the stables to do his share of the milking.

Alone with mother I saw her looking closely at my face: "What a dreadful scar," she said, as she bent over to touch it. "Does it bother you?"

"No, not the scar itself, but I hope later on that a dentist in Stratford can do something about my partial plate; it's loose, you could probably hear the bloody thing clicking as I ate my dinner."

"How many teeth did you lose?"

"Six in the lower right jaw which was broken in two places. That's why I was so long in hospital after I was wounded the first time. They had to wire my jaw together so that it could heal; it took longer than the doctors expected."

"Well," she said, looking at my missing leg, "you're certainly not the young farmer you were five years ago. But I'm so glad you're here with me now. Don't you ever go off to war again!"

"No chance of that," I replied, "I might even be more useful here than in the army. But either way I fear I have little to offer."

"Oh, you may be surprised once you have your new leg. At the least you'll be able to drive the tractor and help me in the house."

Mother, I'm sure, meant well; the idea of usefulness was deeply engrained; she was simply trying to find a role for my abbreviated body. I did not want to discourage her, but a life on a tractor seat or in the house was far from appealing. I was an outside person: crops and cattle close-up were my thing. To change the subject, I asked mother to get the bag that was still attached to my crutch. Once I had it I took out the mink scarf.

"Something especially for you," I said, as I placed the scarf round her neck.

"Oh Jamie, for me! You have been awfully extravagant—but how often I've wanted a fur scarf. And this one is mink and will not be at all like anyone else's at church or in the Women's Institute. What our ladies wear is fox or opossum. But mink . . . is so trim and lovely. Oh, I don't know what to say to you for giving me something so expensive that I wanted."

Then, taking the scarf from her neck, she held it on her lap stroking the fur and saying, "It's so beautiful and see how cleverly the furrier has linked one skin to the other— it's really perfect and all for me. Oh Jamie, thank you very very much."

After she'd replaced the scarf in its wrapping, I thought it a good opportunity to inquire as to how the Old Man was.

"He's certainly not the Old Man he once was," she told me. "He tires easily and complains of stomach and chest pains which he puts down to indigestion and my cooking. What worries me is that he won't go to a doctor; instead he prefers his own prescription, bicarbonate of soda—a teaspoon in half a glass of water which he says always ends his indigestion."

The "Old Man" was a term we often invested father with, not slightingly, but rather as a way to underline his age and his stubborn resistance to change. He was ten years older than Jean his wife, balding, and walked with a stoop his face to the earth as if looking for something he'd lost. But age or his bent body never lessened his authority on our farm; he was always and unmistakably the boss.

"He must be thankful that he has Geoffrey," I told mother. "How capable a man is he?"

"Oh, I do not know how we could survive without him both outside and in. Just look at my hands and these ugly lumps on the knuckles. When my fingers are really red and sore, John will, if he can spare Geoffrey, let me have him for mornings when I have a washing to do."

"How long has he been with you?" I asked.

"Nearly all the time you were Overseas; he's just one of us."

"Why does he walk with a slight limp?"

"He says he broke his leg when he was a boy and that it never healed properly. That misfortune was our good fortune for otherwise like you he would have enlisted. He knows a great deal about the war because I think he's read every book about it that he can get from our local library."

"Is he always as quiet as he was this evening?"

"Oh, he seldom has anything to say which means he gets on swimmingly with your father. Sometimes when he's with me he talks about his early life in England which was not, I gather, an easy one."

And so we chatted on as mother removed the remnants of our dinner and the china from the table to the kitchen, fed the dog, washed the dishes, and put pots and pans to soak in the sink. The two holes in its splasher back were gaping reminders of what mother most wanted in our house—hot and cold running water. Four years in barracks and time in hospitals, where such a convenience was commonplace, made mother's need seem urgent to me.

Beyond the kitchen window a setting sun spilled its light over the stubble of the hay field while cows began their swaying walk away from the stable to the pasture.

On the kitchen wall the sun lit up a small framed scroll; it was my country's tribute to my Uncle Robert who had been killed in what we called the Great War. It was a tribute I knew by heart for my mother had had me memorize it:

> He whom this scroll commemorates was numbered among those who, at the call of King and Country, left all that was dear to them, endured hardness, faced danger, and finally passed out of the sight of men by the path of duty and self-sacrifice, giving up their own lives that others might live in freedom.
> Let those who come after see to it that his name be not forgotten.
>
> Lt. Robert McKay
> Canadian Infantry Bn.

This scroll with its handsome armorial design, topped by Gv R1, circled by *honi soit qui mal y pense* and undergirded by *Dieu et mon Droit* seemed to me as a boy a splendid tribute that brought my King and my very own uncle together in our kitchen. Even as a young man I hoped that I, too, might have a chance to serve my King and country by bearing arms and facing dangers courageously. I do not think I wanted to go so far as giving up my life, but the scroll had been a silent home stimulus when, in June 1940, I enlisted in Uncle Robert's regiment, the Perths. However, as I viewed it now in the sun's fading light, I was no longer stirred, as I had been, by its patriotic abstractions. Its sentiment seemed old-fashioned, questionable.

It was a relief to leave it and go with mother into the farther rooms where she wanted to show me the new sideboard in the dining room that housed the fine china and silver she'd used for our dinner. In the parlour just beyond

I was shown a new chesterfield that she'd covered with a sheet to prevent fading. Our parlour was usually reserved for professional people like the Presbyterian minister or for relatives whom we seldom saw because they lived far away. Its exclusiveness marked our rural status.

"Do you like it?" mother asked anxiously, as she unveiled the chesterfield.

Not wishing to dampen her pride in this acquisition, I told her that it did fit nicely into the room and that I liked the colour. It would, I knew, never serve like the old sofa in the kitchen on which we could stretch out in our farm clothes after a hard day's work in the fields or the barn. Across the hall from the parlour was the bedroom my parents used. A round silvery register in the parlour meant that it was warm in winter when the furnace was going in the cellar. Off the dining room was a smaller room, once intended as a spare bedroom, but now the Old Man's study.

Its central furnishing was a massive roll-top kind of desk which a local carpenter had made to my father's specifications. Its array of locked drawers had always defied my curiosity as a boy. Secrecy cloaked family business. What my parents earned, what they paid for things, what they owed was their business and no one else's. The keys to the desk were so carefully hidden that I never succeeded in finding them. When father worked in his study he was usually alone except on occasion when he needed mother's advice. I never remember her working in it by herself. The room and its desk were the Old Man's sanctum.

With his desk my father had hoped to impose order on his rural affairs. But the study at once revealed how inadequate the desk's numerous drawers and cubbyholes had proved to be for his sense of what should be preserved. Piles of old *Farmer's Advocates* stood by one side of the desk and a mixed bag of farm reports left by Agricultural Representatives—the Ag. Reps.—leaned precariously against the other side. In its disorder the room was the antithesis of mother's parlour. Beyond the study were the stairs which I had always used when going to bed.

"How," asked my mother as she looked at the steep rise, "are you ever going to get up those on your crutches?"

"Don't worry," I told her. "I'll go up"—I almost said on my ass—but remembering in time my mother's aversion to what she called disgusting talk, I substituted "my butt" adding that she could bring up my haversack.

"But," she interjected, "everything would be so much easier if only John had not taken over this spare room. I could," she hesitantly proposed, "have him make room there for a cot for you."

"No, no," I interrupted, "I want to sleep in my own bedroom. I'll get there—you'll see."

The tour of the lower level made, mother insisted I relax in a wicker chair on the verandah where I could rest my stump on a footstool covered, she pointed out, with her own embroidery, a fiery looking rooster. Once I'd settled in to the chair's cushions, she returned to the kitchen to clean up the pots and pans while I sat waiting for the Old Man to come in from the chores.

It was a warm evening with an off-and-on breeze bringing the pungent scent of white clover along the garden fence and, from adjoining fields, the more varied odours of crops not yet harvested. At ease in these good smells of home, I saw a cottontail rabbit hop its way over the lawn to a point just below me where, on a patch of clover, it stretched out and remained for several minutes. Like the rabbit I, too, could relax with no fear of an Orders Group being called on the verandah with map references leading to a rock-lined sangar below Italy's

Monte Cifalco. No need to wait under a hot sun until nightfall for a mess tin of barely warm grub, no need to pee on the stone floor of my cramped living space, no need for prayers in the midst of mortar bursts— just blessed quiet and peace here on our farm.

The Old Man's appearance served further to underline the security of my location for it was his strong brown hands and calculating mind that had shaped this setting, these acres that I knew he had hoped I would work as my own some day. Before he could withdraw his old tobacco pipe from the window ledge, I gave him the new brier one.

"I could use a new pipe," he said in response as he took it from me. "The bowl of my old one is so carboned up that it doesn't hold much tobacco, and I'm afraid I've bitten through the stem."

"Well then, fill this one up so we can see how it burns."

I watched his strong fingers pick bits of Macdonald's fine cut from his pouch, carefully tap them down in the bowl with his index one, and then strike a match to light it up.

"It's a good pipe," he announced as he drew in the smoke. "Nicely balanced, comfortable—thank you Boy. How much did you pay for it?"

"Don't let that worry you," I said. "It's a gift, something I thought you'd appreciate."

"Very kind of you Boy, I needed a new one."

After a pause, while the smoke curled round his tanned lined face, he observed that I'd be anxious "to get this prosthetic thing and see how well you can walk on it."

"Oh, they tell me," I assured him, "that I'll be able to get about reasonably well once the stump is calloused."

The Old Man was anxious to assess my future usefulness on the farm for, as he shifted in his chair to look directly at me, he asked, "How long do you think it will be before you're discharged from the hospital?"

"Not," I told him, "until they're sure I can manage on my own, and that may take some time. The socket has to fit my stump perfectly or it will develop blisters. And I think, too, they are still a bit concerned as to whether they've got all the shrapnel out of my body."

"And who pays the hospital bill?"

"The army or the government—but not me."

"So," he said, drawing in the smoke, "you're not likely to be much help to me by fall—if even then?"

"For goodness sakes, John," exclaimed mother as she joined us, "Jamie's just back and here you are trying to get him working. Do leave him alone. Just be thankful he's here—and not another scroll on the kitchen wall."

His pipe having gone out, the Old Man covered up his reaction to the reprimand by striking another match and getting his pipe lit again. The conversation then shifted to the neighbours, how well they were getting on with the harvesting and who the Logan boy was working for. Here mother interrupted saying that she thought it was time we asked the Logans in for a game of euchre.

"I'd like a visit with Jenny; I haven't seen her daughter Betty in ages, she's in high school now. While I'm catching up on their news, you men can talk about the harvest and the weather."

Ignoring the Logans, father said he was sure no one would be threshing until August. The spring, he told us, had been much too wet. All that he and Geoffrey could do now was to get on with the second cutting of alfalfa.

"What's Geoffrey doing tonight?" I asked, as I'd not seen him since supper.

"Oh, he's seldom with us on a Saturday night," mother replied. "He's down in the village with the softball team; he's the pitcher."

"Might be better off here getting a good night's rest," was the Old Man's rejoinder as he knocked the ash out of his new brier and moved off to his own bed. The nights on our verandah were brief as we all went to bed early in order to rise shortly after five in the morning.

"You must be tired, too, after your train trip," mother said. "Oh dear, I do wish you didn't have to go upstairs and that we had a bathroom. Can't I help you up?"

"No, no help—that's a hospital rule for those of us on crutches; we must learn to be independent. But first I've got to go to the Lilacs."

That necessity over, I left my crutches at the foot of the stairs and went up on the left side of my bottom using my hands and the good leg for propulsion. Before she came up to help me into bed, I even managed to undress and get into my old pyjamas which mother had left on the side of my bed.

"Do you mind," she asked shyly, as she tucked the blanket round me, "if I give you a goodnight kiss?" I put my arms around her neck and drew her down to me as I had done as a little boy. "Oh, Jamie," she whispered, "I'm so glad you're home—even if you can't work on the farm."

The pale yellow light from the coal oil lamp on the commode did not, I hope, enable her to see my full eyes as she kissed the scar and bade me goodnight. That both parents had hoped I could on my return take up my share of the farm work was apparent. They had both in varying measures deplored my service Overseas. Having paid, as it were, this due to their country, they were now disappointed that the compensation came up a leg short. I could understand their disappointment, but I was not prepared to regret what I had done.

But even in the comfort of my bed I could not escape

my missing leg as I imagined the toes wiggling on the foot and felt the distress of phantom pains. Caught up by circumstances of my own choosing, I lay for perhaps a half hour while the sound of crickets drifted in with moonlight through the window. Then sleep slipped its soothing solace over my uneasy mind and body. In a dream I saw Sister Fleda bending over me. She was holding my hands and crying.

In the morning mother brought me a cup of tea and then disappeared to get breakfast for Geoffrey and the Old Man. Slowly I took in the features of a room I'd known for nearly twenty years. Sunshine played over the pattern on the inside wall where a stove pipe hole had been blocked and plastered over. As a child I'd imagined endless scenes suggested by the artistry of a plasterer more accustomed to making a straight furrow than a smooth surface with a trowel.

Now it was 0530 on the morning of January 17, 1944 where a long crack in the plaster served as the Riccio River and an elongated lump beyond, the ridge my company was to seize. I imagined the lump of plaster erupting under the fire of fifteen artillery regiments while my platoon moved off into the river valley in the dull light of an Adriatic dawn. Then I could see my platoon shredded by mortar bursts and machine gun fire.

I was found an hour or so later staggering away from the river bed trying to hold one side of my face together under such pain as I had no idea existed. One of the Perths found me dazed and masked in blood trying to pick teeth out of my mouth. Tying his shell dressing on my face, he took me to a regimental aid post where morphine and ambulances carried me off on a three-month tour of military hospitals. In them I had my lower jaw pinned together, the side of my face and ear stitched up, and finally a partial denture made.

It was the noise of Geoffrey driving the Farmall past the house that put an end to my imaginings and roused me to peace time activities. Dressed, I slid down the stairs to my crutches, said good morning to mother, and made my way to the Lilacs. Back in the kitchen, teetering on one leg with my stump on a chair, I washed hands and face in the sink's wash dish, and dried them on the rough terry towel that hung at the end. Breakfast included hot buttered bannocks smothered with mother's own quince jelly—so unlike what appeared in our army mess tins every morning and a good notch better than the offerings at Christie Street.

Sunday at home passed quietly. We did not go to church to avoid the flight of steps there and the narrow pine pews. Instead, mother and I sat out the morning on the verandah. We were alone as the Old Man and Geoffrey were in the barn caring for one of the Holsteins that was off her feed and keeping an eye on "Old White," the Percheron mare; she was about to foal—probably her last contribution in the face of the competition provided by the Farmall.

"Do you remember walking to school carrying your books and lunch pail?" mother asked as she settled into her chair to finish knitting a toe on a stocking.

"Of course, I do," I replied, "and also those nights when you'd sit with me at the kitchen table and see that my homework was done. Clever of the Old Man to marry a public school teacher!"

Smiling, mother asked, "Do you remember Miss Welsh, your teacher?"

"Oh yes, she was one I really liked."

"Well, I was very surprised last Christmas when I was shopping with my sister at John White's in Woodstock to meet her. She's not changed at all and still so friendly and asked about you very warmly."

Miss Welsh led to talk of my teachers at the Stratford Collegiate. Having met only one of them, my English teacher, mother spoke of her and the amount of supplementary reading she demanded.

"Do you remember," mother added, "reading *Silas Marner* and the talks you and I used to have about it when you'd finished your homework?"

"Of course, I do, and I've never forgotten that rotten Dunsany who staked Wildfire and then stole Silas' hoard of gold guineas. He deserved to drown."

"And the time we spent talking about Godfrey and his Molly and her death in the snow so conveniently close to Silas' cottage?"

"And I still remember," I went on, "how concerned you were that Silas, not Godfrey, should keep Effie."

"Oh yes, and Silas deciding so wisely that there'd be no shrouding of the past and that Effie should be told who her mother was. I've so often thought about his decision."

"Attendance at S.C.V.I. had its advantages, I admit, even though I was always a country boy in its halls envious of the city students."

"What made you envious?"

"Oh, they were or seemed so smart in their dress. They went to the latest movies at the Avon Theatre, knew how to fox trot, and even played tennis, the boys in white trousers, the girls in snowy-white shorts and blouses with sweaters casually looped over their shoulders."

Mother remembered and said she was rather sorry that I'd never been able to take a girl in my classes to a show or a dance. The distance from our place to Stratford was, she pointed out, a drawback and on weekends the Old Man needed my help at home. What mother did not say was that I'd never been allowed to drive the family car until I was in my third year at the Ontario Agricultural College. It was a decree I resented.

Shifting from Stratford but keeping to my lack of a girl friend, mother said it always seemed a mystery to her why I'd never found someone at Macdonald Institute. "After all you were next door to Mac all the four years you spent at the O.A.C."

To quiet mother's curiosity on this subject, I told her I had been a bit of a slow boat and overly conscientious. Whatever truth rested in this self-portrayal, dodged the question. Although the Ontario Agricultural College was completely male dominated, we were all aware that just across the campus was to be found an interesting variety of girls many of whom were from country homes. What I was not prepared to tell my mother were details of an outing I had in my last year that ended ignominiously in the woods back of the Veterinary College.

She was an attractive, somewhat boisterous Mac senior, not at all averse to dalliance among the trees. Trouble was she found my fumbling, ill-adjusted technique so outrageous on her person that reassembling her clothing she marched off in sullen silence refusing to be consoled. Sadly the news of my prurient gambit filtered down to my year in Upper Hunt where, for the rest of the term, I suffered from much scurrility. Ignorant of this fiasco, mother assured me I was not a slow boat and said she was sure I'd have no trouble finding a good mate.

I recognized the sense, even the urgency that underlay mother's suggestion. What I had to overcome for many years was a kind of delicate hang-up. Girls had become, from primary school on, creatures who were to be respected. "No rough house or else!" I came to view them through high school as too pretty, too decorous to treat carnally. In their cotton frocks and frilly blouses they existed in a kind of forbidden romantic landscape. A smile or an affectionate word from one of them was enough to render me quite ineffectual. And two escapades

Overseas with street ladies indifferent to propriety or technique did little to render me more accomplished.

And yet my father, in his fancied role as patriarch, had several times in my late teens pointed me in what he regarded as a sensible marital direction. Usually his advice was tendered after he had heard of some young man of no prospects who had coupled successfully with an equally indigent maiden.

"Just you don't be so damned silly," he'd shout in the barn, jabbing a calloused finger toward me. "Find a decent country girl with some family backing. And don't come home with some blonde who can't tell a turnip from a mangel. What you'll need is a farmer's daughter with a straight back, clean legs, deep chested . . ." Here, rather alarmed at his reliance upon the appearance of a prize Holstein for the essential qualities of a daughter-in-law, he'd drop the subject with his favourite command: "Just use your common sense, Boy."

Moving off on the train from Stratford on Monday morning left me relieved. Although I was pleased I had renewed links with my mother and father, I had become aware of how much they had expected of me and how disappointed they must have been to find a part of me missing—a part that rendered my active service on the farm of doubtful value. As the miles clicked off the train's wheels, I was aware, too, that to spend the rest of my life on the 3rd Concession might not be as appealing as once I'd imagined. A life of pulling milk seven days a week from Holsteins, of pinching pennies, and accepting the freaks of weather in all seasons had about it a kind of sad resignation. Toronto's Union Station that day seemed a gateway to a wider more attractive existence.

Chapter 3

Perplexing Matters

"Well Boy, how did you find the folks back on the farm? Were they pleased to see you?" It was Nursing Sister Fleda now on days. With me on my stomach, she was removing the surgical dressing from my buttock.

"It has healed nicely," she announced. "All it needs now is a small patch, but it's been such a slow process that I wonder if you're not still hanging on to some pieces of old iron inside you." Later, as she looked at my stump, she concluded that the weekend at home provided the very medicine I needed: "You're ready for a prosthesis any time now." Then, as she tidied my bed, she inquired, "What did your mother have to say when she saw you on crutches?"

"Not much, she was more upset because the house still lacks a three-piece bathroom and because of the steep stairs that lead to my bedroom."

"And did you manage to get up and down?"

"Oh yes, it wasn't at all difficult."

"Why don't you suggest that she and your father come to Toronto for a weekend? I'd like to meet your mother. They could stay at the Royal York which is not far from here and have a holiday as well as see you. The meals at the Royal York are really something, and I'm sure they'd be comfortable."

"A good idea , Sister, but you don't know my father. He'd balk at the cost and at the same time say he couldn't leave the milking and all the chores to the hired man especially now when there's so much to do on the land."

"But don't they ever get away from the farm?"

"Not really unless you count the occasional day shopping in town or once a year for a day at the Stratford fair. Cows are very demanding creatures and have to be milked twice a day every day of the week."

"So I may never see your mother, what a pity!"

"Not likely at all," I replied. "At this time of the year she's regarded as an essential cog in the farm's operation. The men expect her to produce meals three times a day, care for their bruises and cuts, do the laundry, mend their clothes, keep the house tidy, and—in emergencies—even help with the milking."

"That seems unfair to me—so it does."

"But," I countered venturesomely, "what's wrong with your coming home with me for a weekend as soon as my new leg is properly fitted?"

"That's sweet of you Boy, but I have two or three medical appointments coming up sometime soon so I should stay in the city and," she added, "whatever would your busy mother think if you brought me to her door? 'Some nerve she has!' I can imagine her saying. And I wouldn't know how to behave. I've never in my life been on a farm."

Our mutual proposals ended as she responded to a call from No Arms and then moved away to other beds. Later at the end of her shift she told me that I could expect a technician in the next day to measure me for a new leg.

That afternoon we were visited by a phalanx of earnest elderly ladies in smartly tailored suits, saucy felt hats, and carrying large leather handbags. They served us tea with small sandwiches, cakes, and cookies. They were solicitous about our welfare, anxiously sympathetic, facing our physical shortcomings with maternal aplomb. One of them stopped to inquire about me.

"And what," she asked smiling, as she took a two-pound box of Eaton's Cottage chocolates and a carton of cigarettes from her handbag, "happened to you?"

Sitting in my chair by the side of my bed, I thought the lack of a leg rendered her question unnecessary, and I was tempted to ask if she'd seen an optometrist lately, but I reined in my rudeness not wanting to forfeit the chocolates on my bed. These came my way sometimes because I did not smoke. So I told her I was first wounded in Italy.

"And where," she interrupted, "were you in hospital?" On hearing me say "Altamura first and then Andria," somewhat startled she said, "Why Andria is where my husband served as a surgeon. You may have met him, Dr. John Symonds."

Admitting that I did not remember the name, our conversation from then on was less restrained as she told me that her husband had first served in the Advanced Dressing Station in Ortona where I had had my face wounds dressed. But clouded by morphine and the confusion of stretcher cases, I had no memory of who attended me at that time. Patting my hands and tendering the chocolates, Mrs. Symonds said she'd certainly mention my name to her husband and assured me she'd come another time to see me.

"I cannot," she said, "tell you when because August is the month when John and I hope to holiday in Muskoka." As it turned out, I never saw Mrs. Symonds again, but I did enjoy the chocolates she left with me.

The next afternoon an agreeable prosthetics technician arrived to see how well my stump had healed and to take the necessary measurements saying he was certain the new leg would be ready before the coming weekend. He had barely left the ward when Far Bed waving *The Globe and Mail* demanded our attention:

"Say you guys, guess what! We've picked up another

V.C., and he's on his way home now without any legs. Anyone here from the Essex Scottish?"

"Here, Sir!" came from the blind man with no arms lying half asleep on his bed who added truculently: "What's wrong with the Essex? No better lot of foot sloggers in the 2ⁿᵈ Div. We were on the beaches in Normandy while you guys were swanning about in sunny Italy."

"Poor bugger never heard of Sicily—a full year before he hit the beaches," Gunner remarked.

Ignoring the interruption, Far Bed told No Arms that the V.C. was an Essex officer.

"Well, who is it, what's his name?" demanded No Arms now fully awake.

"Says here in the paper, he's a Major Fred Tilston."

"Good God!" shouted No Arms pounding his heels on his bed, "he was my company officer—and a damned good one, too; everyone liked old Fred, he looked after us and was always right with us when we went in on the Jerries. I'm glad he's got old Vicky's gong. Where were the Essex when it happened?"

"Well, if you'll shut up I'll read what the *Globe* has to say."

"Oh, just get on with it, we're not deaf," exclaimed No Arms.

"All right, all right, I hear you . . . It was west of the Rhine on the first of March at the edge of the Hochwald Forest where the Germans were dug in—and if you'll let me read—this is what it says: 'Major Tilston, although wounded, led his company through wire and was the first man on the Germans taking one prisoner. Then he was wounded again but held the position in the face of counter attacks despite the loss of three-quarters of his men. Then he was wounded a third time when the company's last surviving officer took over. Tilston's example,' this article concludes, 'gave his brigade a solid base for clearing the Jerries out of the Hochwald'."

"Wonder what he'll do now without legs?" asked No Arms. "Hope he can see what's left of them."

In reply from behind the newspaper we heard Far Bed say, "Apparently he wants to return to the office job he had in Windsor before the war, so he must have his eyesight. But he's thirty-eight years old—he's getting on—and he's a bachelor."

"Yeah, that's our old Fred," No Arms added. "He'll make out if anyone will, and I hope he finds a sensible woman who'll care for him."

The paper eventually made its rounds as we reviewed the war news until supper put an end to explanation and argument. In the evening we listened to *Amos n'Andy* over CFRB. We laughed much and accepted Far Bed's critique of the program: "Those niggers sure are funny as hell, ain't they?"

Two days later the technician brought my leg which seemed to fit my stump comfortably. It was a strange feeling to stand again on two feet, the ward applauding as with a cane in my right hand and Sister Fleda on my left side, I managed to walk from one end of the ward to the other and then down the hall to another nursing station. Sister roundly praised my performance saying all I needed was a pair of matching shoes. I was, however, left with a distinct impression of how unlike my own leg the pros-thesis was and how much effort it took to move it at all naturally.

But before the weekend, I was gaining in confidence as I went back and forth to the lavatory and even to our small library where I sat and talked to Gunner. We were alone. We had much to share because he had been raised on a Saskatchewan farm and had enlisted to escape the effects of the Great Depression. His unit, the RCHA, belonged to the 1st Division which meant that his tour in

Italy was longer than mine. But, it was about farming we talked and what our prospects were if we returned to make a living on our farms. Gunner was adamant:

"Not a damned hope—even if they find out here what's wrong with me. I've had more than enough of drought, dust storms, and bloody cold winters. I'm off to Vancouver Island the first chance I get."

"And what'll you do there?" I asked.

"I'll get a job in a sawmill or in the woods for a beginning. The only good thing about farming is that you're your own boss, but debts and a patched ass on the prairies are not for me."

I explained to him how matters stood with me at home and the drawback of a peg leg.

"Well, hell," he said, "you're lucky, you have a college degree, you can forget about farming. Get a government job in town: nine to four, five days a week, and take a fat pension at the end of the road. You got it made, forget about pulling tits seven days a week."

Gunner's blunt assessment of farming as a suitable vocation for either of us left me more uncertain than ever about my Zorra inheritance. What I had set my mind on before the war was the pleasure of days in the sun planting and harvesting my own fields and the close management and caring for prize cattle. That prospect dimmed as I observed the limitations imposed by a missing leg. What I needed now was more time to consider, more time at home where I could assess the odds—and my parents.

If the daylight hours sometimes left me disturbed, even confused, my nights, too, contributed a share of distress. Tired and dusty, I was all too often, Tommy gun clutched tight, rounding a corner in an Italian town and almost running into a German paratrooper who stood holding his hand out to me. Refusing his gesture, asking no questions, I fired and watched his blue-grey jacket bob in and out as he crumpled, his Mauser clattering on the cobblestones. Then kneeling beside him, I took his hand and told him I was sorry I'd been so quick on the trigger.

The awakening from this dream was as troubling as the dream itself for I had killed a young German paratrooper at close range on a street corner in Ceprano, but he had never held out a hand of friendship. Perhaps it was his astonishment at seeing the sweat-streaked scar on my face that was his undoing for, as he glanced, I fired.

My mistake lay not in the death I'd meted him—this after all was what I was supposed to do. The mistake I made was standing over a youth and seeing the pale down of his unshaven lip and chin, his clenched teeth, his pleading eyes, and his hands clutching his belly while blood bubbled over the *Gott mit Uns* on his belt buckle. I should not have looked. Over this killing a miasma of dream and reality by night and day often made me miserable.

In the ward I welcomed the diversions that took my mind off that Ceprano street corner in the Liri Valley or, for that matter, off the Zorra farm I was to inherit. Nearly every afternoon our ward was a kaleidoscope of nurses, orderlies, doctors, and visitors coming and going in contrast to us wounded who remained and gave the place a kind of permanence. Nothing unusual about impermanence as I thought of my past. Four years in the Perths and where were the hundreds of us with whom I'd boarded the *Reina del Pacifico* in the Halifax harbour on October 5, 1941? Many of them certainly in cemeteries in Italy and the Netherlands. The rest? A few of us in military hospitals, the others scattered across the thousands of miles of Canadian landscape.

Permanence for me should have been a future farming my own land. My weekend at home had sensibly linked me to my own folk: a mother, father, a dead uncle. They should have been in regimental terms my support com-

the work."

"Do you still make those rolls?"

"Of course I do! They were the first thing I decided to bake when I heard you were coming. As soon as we get this washing on the line, you shall try them with butter." Later with the laundry drying under the warm August sun, we did sit out on the verandah and had tea and rolls much to my comfort as I thought of the store-bought cookies that went with tea at the hospital. Memories of the past on the farm crowded out Christie Street and even my service with the Perths as mother and I talked out the morning. To our right we could see Geoffrey tedding the second cutting of alfalfa on our front field. "Old White," the Belgian, was pulling the tedder. In an adjoining field we could see father at work in the corn with a team.

"Haying this year," mother said, "has been later than usual because we had so cold and wet a spring."

"But what's the Old Man doing in the corn?" I asked.

"Oh that's something new that does away with hoeing. You can see, if you look closely, that the corn has been planted running both lengthwise and crosswise in the field so that it can be cultivated both ways. Your father sits on the cultivator and even uses his feet to manoeuvre the teeth. The Percherons soon learn to keep within the rows."

"That's better than hoeing," I said, "for I still remember my aching shoulder and blistered hands on June weekends. I thought those rows of corn endless."

"Oh, changes do take place," mother observed, "but if only we had the hydro—that's what I want more than anything. No more trying to keep milk from souring in the basement, no more coal oil lamp globes to clean, no more blacking and polishing the McClary, or pulling and pushing on the washer. And you can have no idea how badly I want hot and cold running water and a three-piece bath—that would be heaven!"

On the subject of hydro we saw eye to eye. "And it would be," I added, "a great help in the barn, especially if father could get a milking machine."

"I'm sure you're right although John thinks getting us equipped in both house and barn will be too expensive. But on the house, however, I've no intention of giving in to his cautious frugality."

"Good for you—just stick to your guns—he'll give way eventually. By the way, how many cows are milking now?"

"Fifteen—he and Geoffrey share the chore twice a day. That's what keeps us here year long—prisoners with no hope of parole."

"And what hope is there," I asked, "that the provincial government will bring hydro along the 3rd Concession?"

"Oh, they're talking as usual," mother replied, "although just a few days ago our Mr. Drew—he's the Premier—pledged to get hydro out to Ontario's back concessions—which is certainly where we are."

To cheer her I pointed out that as people in Embro and Harrington had hydro she might not have long to wait. "And when it does come," I said, "I'll bankroll you for any appliances you want."

"That's good of you Jamie to be so generous, but we do have our own savings, and I'll certainly badger your father to spend them on what we really need."

Shifting away from hydro, I asked what plans father had for the farm which was just one hundred acres that included ten of bush.

"Oh," mother replied, "I don't think I've told you. Last year he leased the Logan farm—that's another eighty acres and a lot of extra work. But John thought he could manage with Geoffrey until your return—but now—he's disappointed and, I think, worried although he won't admit it. We were both counting on you. As you know, he was seventy on his last birthday, and it's time he slowed down."

As it was now nearly eleven o'clock, we had to leave off talk. Mother gathered up the tea things and went at once to the kitchen to prepare dinner leaving me immersed in a flood of associations as I remembered the farm and its animals when I was a boy: the Holsteins aligned in their stanchions, the calves in the box stalls, the horses at the far end of the barn, the silo from which we forked out ensilage, the great white and black bull with the golden ring in his nose, the clanking sound of the manure carrier behind the cows, even the barn cat sitting so composed with her tail tucked round her waiting for a saucer of foaming warm milk. I always thought the barn more interesting than the house for it responded so splendidly to the seasons as it was filled and emptied. It offered a continuum of learning not always, I discovered, without mishap.

One morning at milking time, when I may have been five or six, I saw the cat outside the milk house. I wanted to catch it, but cat did not want boy. Running to get it, I saw it race through the open stable door. In full pursuit I followed it down behind the cows where just ahead of me it turned sharp left through an empty stall. I braked disastrously on the slippery concrete, spun half round and fell in the gutter behind a cow which, having fed on green grass, had left a pool of shiny manure awaiting my arrival.

Circumstances were far from favourable, for milking that cow was the Old Man. The cow was a nervous three-year-old not at all accustomed to confusion. As I fell she jumped and put a hind foot in the foaming pail. That's when I heard a Jehovah-like voice thunder: "God almighty Boy, what are you doing?" Throwing his three-legged stool to one side, the milk pail in one hand and me in the other by what he called the ass of my pants, father carried me dangling to the door of the milkhouse where he dropped me and the pail while he took the hose from the cooling tank and turned it on my filth. That done he stripped me of my trousers and shirt, slapped my bottom, and sent me off in tears to the house. Astonished by my appearance, mother, on hearing what had happened, washed and clothed me and warned me to stay in the house for the rest of the day.

Other of my barn experiences were memorably pleasant—even sweet scented. Of these haying was for me a spectacle which I had to witness standing on the gangway so as to be out of harm's way. From this vantage point I could watch and envy the Old Man, crouched low over the front rack, drive the Percherons hauling a huge load of dry clover and timothy on to the barn floor. At the same time my mother would bring "Old White," the mare, up the gangway to be hitched to a whippletree that was attached to a big rope that ran far back into the barn. While this was going on, father would take a small trip rope in his hands to pull a trolley with a fork hanging from it along the track below the barn's peak to where it locked above his head and let the fork drop down to his hands that drove it deep into the hay. Bouncing his weight on the fork's cross bar, he'd then pull a handle up that hooked the fork into the hay. Standing clear and holding the trip rope, he'd shout to mother who, tapping the reins on "Old White's" back would set off down the gangway. Almost at once the whippletree would rise above "White's" heels and her traces tighten against her collar as she took up her end of the big rope that mysteriously sent a huge bundle of hay swinging out of my sight to the barn's peak where it snapped on to the trolley and sped off into the dusky light of the hay mow where father would trip it sending it down to a waiting hired man who would spread it.

For a five-year-old boy it was activity to marvel at, and I always hoped for the special treat of being lifted up on the empty wagon for the trip to the hayfield, my bare feet dangling from the edge of the rack and, like the hired man, chewing on a stem of timothy. Here I was with men whose hay-making abilities I envied with all my being— just to stand under the loader before those tumbling swaths of clover and timothy and fork them back to father —that for me then was the chief end of man.

And I did as I grew up become more than a spectator, first taking my mother's place behind "Old White," then perched on the rack at the wagon's front driving the Percherons. A few years later, the boyish vision became reality, when, streaked with sweat, I was at the loading end forking to the hired man while the Old Man drove the Farmall instead of the Percherons. I was now a man—as those on West Zorra farms knew the meaning of the word —and proud I was of the rank which I now fear an air burst shell over Holwierde has taken from me forever.

Mother's call to dinner put an end to recollection and demotion. Dinner at the kitchen table still had its usual pattern: listening to the news over our battery powered Viking radio, inquiring about the neighbours who may have telephoned, and hearing the Old Man's comments on the headlines of *The Globe and Mail* which he'd retrieved from the roadside mail box and scanned on his way to the house. An hour later Geoffrey and father would be off to the fields, and I would be left with mother.

Later that week I managed with my cane to walk out to the barn despite the uneven laneway and the drag of my right foot. At the barn I met the Old Man coming in with the Percherons. I wanted, as in the past, to help him un-hitch, but as I couldn't bend over to unhook the traces I waited and with my left hand took the near horse by his bridle intending to go with him to the watering trough. It was a foolish move as the horse knowing what he wanted shook his head and moved off quickly. I lost my balance and fell. After getting me up on my feet, my father's only remark made clear my inadequacy:

"You've a long way to go Boy before you can be much use to me on this farm."

His observation was in its bareness and truth one I much resented at the time because I had become accustomed to hearing Nursing Sister Fleda praise me for the progress I was making. This blunt assessment was right on target and hurt. So not replying, I left my father to the chores and returned to the house resolving enroute to prove that I could be useful, given an opportunity.

That evening before supper I heard father tell Geoffrey that he wanted him to take the tractor and wagon in the morning to continue clearing up a fence line at the far end of the farm. He could not help Geoffrey as he had to go to Embro to have some welding done at the blacksmith's. Here, I thought, was opportunity.

The next morning, after the Old Man had left, I told the taciturn Geoffrey that I was going with him and that I'd drive the tractor. Once I was helped up into the seat, the driving was easy because the gas was adjusted at the steering wheel, and I could brake and clutch using my left foot. The morning went well, and by noon Geoffrey had picked up much of the trash along the fence line leaving only a few piles of stone. The trash I hauled off to an old stone pile where Geoffrey pitched it off the wagon.

Back at the barn at noon, as Geoffrey gave me a hand down from the Farmall, my right buttock felt tender. This I put down to the weeks of sitting and lying about that I'd done in hospitals waiting for healing to take place. But I did decide the next time to take something soft to cushion the bucket-shaped seat on the Farmall. The rest of that day I spent on the cushions of the wicker chair on the verandah reading back numbers of *The Globe and Mail*, a daily extravagance the Old Man accepted both for its detailed market reports and for its conservative bias which appealed to his understanding of what government should be about.

I did not share his enthusiasm for his daily paper finding its editorials dull and the comics, save for the occasional "Blondie," not at all as amusing as the "Herbie" cartoons in the *Maple Leaf*. I did read the war news—one could not miss the accounts of the *Queen Mary*, the *Acquitania*, the *Louis Pasteur*, the *Lady Nelson*, and the *Letitia* bringing Canadians home from Europe. But I remained strangely unmoved by the war in the Pacific. It was not my war. I could not imagine its enormous scale: the great naval battles, the vast armadas of Superforts, and the massive assaults on little known remote islands in the Pacific.

My mind ran very much on myself: to phantom pains in a missing leg and foot, to a lad I'd killed, to five months in hospitals, to the inadequacies of a prosthesis, and to the Old Man's appraisal of my usefulness. These inner concerns were set back on August 7 when I saw the paper's stark black headlines: ATOMIC BOMB ROCKS JAPAN. Even the allied bombing of Berlin, Hamburg, and Cologne seemed less awful than this new weapon that could in one drop nearly blot out an entire city. It was the paper said, "the greatest force ever discovered by man."

"All to the good," father said. "That should bring the Japs to their senses and an end to this war that's been dragging on all too long."

"But," mother cried, "just think of all the women and children huddled beneath such a blast. Oh, this war is so awful!"

"Not much we can do about, is there?" was

Geoffrey's cryptic remark as he set out for the stables.

"At least," I said, "it may not be necessary now to send Canadians to the Pacific—and maybe we can get our Hong Kong boys home."

Pushing his chair back from the table, the Old Man delayed following Geoffrey as he went on reading.

"I see," he noted, "that the Liberals in Ottawa have come to their senses. They're now offering to pay the full cost of Old Age Pensions to all of us over seventy regardless of how much money we're making. Can't say," he went on, "that $30.00 a month is enough to live on but for the elderly, who are poor, it'll help. Wonder when I'll get my first cheque."

Just then Geoffrey tapped on the door to find out if the Old Man could help him get the binder out of the drive-shed where it had been stored until needed. No more family conversation took place until supper time and evening when my father and I were together on the verandah. Once he had his new pipe lit, he observed that the addition of the Logan acres to our farm meant that we could—if we had the help—increase our milk production.

"Do you think," he asked, "that your new leg will let you get down to milk a cow—it's not a good place to have a fall, you know?"

"Oh I imagine I can risk it, although it might be a bit tricky getting out from under with a full pail of milk."

"Well," he went on, "if we have more cows we need help for the milking." Then, talking through the smoke that eddied about his face, he startled me with a suggestion.

"What you'll need Boy is a strong, straight-backed woman, the kind who knows how to milk a cow and look after you. You can find one or two locally who'd fit the bill, but you'll have to get on the ball."

As she moved out to us from cleaning up in the

kitchen, mother had intercepted her husband's suggestion. "And just what sort of ball game John is this you're recommending? Whatever makes you think that one of our local girls would just love to milk cows morning and night as well as make meals and do all the housework? Or were you leaving some of the housework for me? Whatever has happened, John, to your common sense? Jamie is quite capable of deciding on a wife himself. And he doesn't need a milkmaid."

Not wishing to challenge mother, who nearly always could best him in an argument, the Old Man knocked the ash from his pipe on the verandah rail and surprised me by asking if I could next morning help Geoffrey clear away the rest of the stones on the fence line. "He can," he said, "get on much faster if someone's driving the tractor."

Having deflected his wife's criticism of his marital plan for me and on hearing my willingness to drive the tractor, he announced it was his bedtime and went off to the kitchen where we heard a glass being taken from the cupboard.

"There," mother whispered, "he's into the bicarbonate of soda again. I do wish he'd see a doctor about his indigestion."

"Why don't you simply make an appointment for him?"

"That's an idea," she replied, "although he'll be hopping mad when he finds out. Doctors, he's always maintained, are expensive, and all they do is make out prescriptions for pharmacists who charge too much for little boxes of pills."

"Then let's telephone the first of next week," I said.

"All right—and you remind me Jamie."

The question settled for the time we sat longer than usual to watch a horned moon rise over our maples as

stars shyly graced its orbit. Without a preface I heard
mother say quietly:

> The moving Moon went up the sky,
> And nowhere did abide:
> Softly she was going up,
> And a star or two beside.

"And where," I asked, "did you find those lines?

"Oh, years ago; I memorized them for a test—I forget
which one—maybe it was in Grade XII or in Normal
School. It was a long poem in a little green book edited,
if I remember correctly, by someone named Stevenson—I
still have it somewhere."

"What was Stevenson's first name?" I asked.

"Oh, we girls giggled about it when someone told
us—Orlando, so romantic!"

"Then I'm certain that's the person I had for an
English course at Guelph. We called him Doc Steevie."

"What was he like?"

"An old man, rather stooped. He used to trot across
the campus with a little dog he took to his office in
Massey Hall. He was different. He'd bring recordings of
classical music to his lectures, play them on an old
gramophone for us, and often talk about art and Canadian
authors. Not all the Aggies liked him, but I did, and I
remember he included 'The Rime of the Ancient Mariner'
in the course."

"And here we are," mother said, "just you and I
watching a rising moon and seeing not one or two but a
host of stars round about it. A night like this in the country puts a sort of halo round the day's hard work."

Her remark, as I thought about it later in bed, was
clear evidence of an artistic sense that some thirty years
of household drudgery had not effaced. It was evidence,
too, of why I always preferred my mother's mind to my

father's. His unceasing attention to his land and the beasts thereon was in the end more impairing than my mother's acceptance of housework. While striving single-mindedly to make a living and to make sure he had a successor, he lost the sense of wonder that all children inherit. His horizon was close in and always recognizable. No moving moon endued his bedtime.

The next day Geoffrey, with me cushioned on the Farmall's seat, finished clearing up the fence line of stones. By evening I was again aware of pain in my rump as if I'd been sitting on broken glass and wished Fleda were near to have a peek at the trouble spot. As a result, for the next ten days or so I stayed off the tractor and, aside from walks out and back from the stables, spent most of my time in the house helping mother who treated me often as a little boy to be rewarded with cookies for slight services rendered. Father had little to say to me. No man worth his salt spent his days in doors with womenfolk on a farm. The house was out-of-bounds save for meals and a pause before bed time. Hospitality, of course, required exceptions.

On two occasions we were invited to visit neighbours: the McKay Bhards and the Murrays who had told mother they very much wanted to see me. I remember those evenings because of how little the neighbours were interested in hearing about my travels and life within a regiment. Once they were assured that I was in flesh the McKay Black's boy they had known four years before and had learned about my leg, questions about the war never arose. They fastened on the local agenda: the coming municipal elections, the need to gravel our road, township drainage, and proposals for a consolidated school system. Once these issues had been aired, we relaxed over a substantial lunch before returning home. I suspect there was good reason for the little interest in my wartime doings.

For over four years these neighbours had been inundated with newspaper and radio accounts of the horrors. My platoon's long route marches and dawn assaults on enemy strong points could only now be prosaic alongside the enduring realities of existence in West Zorra.

It was mother who insisted we have the Logans in for an evening. We had, of course, known them for years. Charles Logan had lost much of the use of his left arm in a car accident in 1939. Finding it increasingly difficult over the war years to go on farming, he'd been willing to lease his acres to the Old Man. Jenny Logan, his wife, was in mother's language "a good soul" who had faced the urgencies of farm life and childbirth with courage and consistent good humour. Mother cited her frequently as a rural exemplar.

One of Jenny's two sons was married and lived in Hamilton. The other boy, Lorne, had finished school and was working by the day for farmers who needed his strong arms and back. He could not be with us that evening as he was with Geoffrey in the village on the softball team. Jenny's third child, Betty, came with her parents. I remembered her as a gangling eleven-year-old before the war, shy and awkward. Now as she came in with her parents I was really surprised.

She was almost as tall as I, filled out impressively, with a mop of red hair and a smile as engaging as her greeting. She was wearing blue farmerette cotton overalls the bib of which curved out enticingly. A striped shirtwaist and moccasin-type Oxfords finished her off top and bottom. Overall, on first glance she seemed one the Old Man might accept as a daughter-in-law if she were proposed as such.

With greetings over the parents wasted no time getting down to their favourite pastime, a game of euchre on the dining room table. It was a diversion for which the

Old Man was always willing to sacrifice two hours of his bedtime. As a player I had always been a disappointment so no chance of my being asked to play.

Aware of me on my crutches, Mrs. Logan said, "Betty do you think you can find something to do with Jamie? You mustn't stand watching us, and Jamie will want to sit." Whether mother and daughter had discussed this possibility beforehand, I had no way of knowing, but it was Betty who turned her dimpling face to me with a suggestion.

"Did you ever play cribbage?"

"Yes," I told her, "many times in the army when we were in quiet areas with little to do."

"Would you like to play with me?"

"Sure, but I'm certain there's no cribbage board in this house."

"Don't worry," she said. "Hang on a minute, I've got one in the car."

A few minutes later she appeared with board, pegs, and a pack of cards. We then took over the kitchen table and got down to play. Almost as soon as I watched her brown strong hands shuffle, deal, lay out, and heard the order to "cut," I sensed this attractive red head was no novice at the game. Turning up a knave, she cheerfully declared "two for his heels" and we were away. But it was in tallying a hand that she really impressed me. None of my adding slowly up pairs, fifteens, and runs. Betty's brown eyes flicked over her hand and crib and then at once she had the score. Well ahead of me on the board after four lay outs, she eased up and teased.

"Oh Jamie, if you're not careful you're going to lose your drawers! You'll have to do better or I'll skunk you."

And not surprisingly—for the goddess of chance certainly favoured her hands—she did just that. In game two I escaped that disgrace but realized more and more my partner's cunning. Game three was memorable. We were neck in neck nearing the home stretch when she turned up a 5 of hearts and then expressed delight as I'd never heard so phrased.

"Well jiggle my headlights and open your eyes, Jamie. Take a look at what I have to offer and surrender!"

She held in her hand three 5's and the knave of hearts for 29, the highest possible score. It was a hand I'd heard about but never witnessed in play. The jiggle of her overall's bib and her laughter audibly and visually celebrated her quota of good luck. Deciding that further play would be only an anticlimax and another defeat for me we sat and talked.

Conversation revealed that she and her brother were cribbage addicts and had played the game for years, that she was beginning her sixteenth year, and that following Grade XII she planned to take a secretarial course so that she could get a job in town.

"But what's wrong with the country?" I asked. "You could, I'm sure, find and marry a young farmer."

"Are you serious?" she asked.

"Of course, isn't it a good idea?"

"Not for this kid, it isn't. I've had enough of country living. Give me a break! No, Jamie," she countered, "I'm for a nice apartment in town, electric washer, frig and all, and an office job—and no smelly cows to milk."

As Betty unwittingly shot down one of the Old Man's marital notions for me, mother arrived to demand the kitchen as it was time for food. Betty and I moved off to the dining room where her mother asked about the cribbage and heard about Betty's perfect hand. Smiling roguishly, Betty assured the euchre fans that she had loved being able to play with me and hoped we could do so another time. Sandwiches and a chocolate layer cake sent all of us off to our night's rest. In my bed awake I thought of Betty's bouncing bib and, as the phantom pains made themselves felt, of Nursing Sister Fleda on her rounds. Later I dreamed of escorting a pretty girl with red hair to our barn to help me milk our Holsteins.

The next day on the verandah, as I reviewed my days and nights on the 3rd Concession, I sensed that all was not as solid as I one time thought. A one-hundred acre farm was now not enough for us or for our neighbours. Electrified towns and cities and their conveniences beckoned to country young folk like the Logans. And I thought, too, that the overall rural structure, so obvious in our one-room schools and township councils, faced change—not yet always apparent but threatened.

Here at home the security I had taken for granted was uncertain, even elusive. My missing leg meant I had forfeited the expectations of my rural past and placed a hazard on the gilded future. I was an outsider barely able to grow my own pottage and without the keys to the secrets of a locked desk. I was open to the charge of having been dim-witted, of having sold my birthright for an ideal still realized only imperfectly.

As always this day and others drifted away to their dusky horizons when even war's vivid images began to fade in mind. One exception to this easeful drift did occur. It happened during a storm that came up late on a hot afternoon when I was with Geoffrey in the barn. I'd quite forgotten how menacing these storms could be as the west darkened over the horizon and thunder like distant divisional artillery warned of the deceptive calm followed by wind, and torrential rain, and jagged lightning that laced the sky overhead. The rolling distant thunder merged into a cacophony of vicious cracks that had the scary timbre of German 88's.

And how comforting it was to lean on the lower half of a stable door and watch and hear the storm threaten us.

Comforting especially as I remembered just a year before
how four days of storm and rain brought the Perths to a
standstill in front of the Fiumicino River along the
Adriatic where so many of my platoon were killed. Comforting, too, as I recalled how cold, and wet, and muddy
I was as I sheltered in slit trenches dug in heavy, sticky
clay that so effectively hindered our armour from break-
ing out into the Po Valley.

"I guess," said Geoffrey, as the storm moved off to
the east, "that this noise and lightning must remind you of
the war."

"It surely does Geoffrey. You can't imagine how
good it is to be dry and safe beside you in this barn."

With nothing more to say the reticent Geoffrey went
off with Caesar to get the cows, and I made my way to
mother who wanted to know why I'd sheltered in the barn
and left her in the house. She had grown accustomed to
my being near at hand while my backside and stump
continued to trouble me sitting or standing.

As my days with mother in the house were notably
free of anxiety or commotion, the drift of time was only
apparent on the calendar. But the drift took on emphasis
in black ink on August 14 as father waved the front page
of his paper at us over the dinner table.

"What did I tell you?" he declared. "The Japs have
thrown in the towel, they're licked and a damned good
thing. Thank God we used the atom bomb on them!"

We could all see the bold headlines on the front page,
JAPANESE QUIT as the Old Man read some of the
editorial to us praising the aptness of its title, "A Divine
Decision." I was tempted to say that such reference might
embarrass the Almighty when I remembered the *Gott mit
Uns* on the belt buckle of the lad I shot—and was silent.
Mother, too, said nothing as we let the Old Man finish the
editorial and saw him set off for the stables safe at last

from the Japs.

In the week ahead house routine, shopping in Stratford, and mother's decision to paper the kitchen served to take my mind off the burned women and children of Hiroshima. Helping, too, was the distress I felt when sitting even on a cushioned chair and the suspicion that blisters were forming on my stump. The distress persuaded me to make an appointment at 352 Christie Street which Admissions eventually arranged for me on Wednesday, August 22, telling me that I should be there for several days.

As that day neared, I began to look forward to the change. The Old Man's obvious unrest over my inadequacies was unsettling and the round of my house chores boring. I was both a part and not a part of the farm's vital life. And I found both father and mother less than forthright at times, not at all willing, for example, to apprise me of financial records so securely kept in the roll-top desk. I was not even told the terms of the lease on the Logan land, although I admit I had not plainly asked. But despite mother's anxiety to please me and a sort of grudging acceptance by her husband, I was beginning to think of myself as a non-paying guest whose time was running out.

To settle in to my seat on the CN's Stratford–Toronto run brought both a feeling of relief and pain—relief to be beyond the parental orbit and pain that one of mother's cushions failed to ease unless I leaned over on the left side of my bottom end. No doubt about it I needed some medical attention.

Chapter 5

Fleda

"And what's your name? You've been here before, haven't you?"

I'd just arrived back at 352 Christie as the nurse on duty in my old ward was making up her charts.

"What seems to be wrong?" she asked.

"A sore behind and blisters on my stump."

"Well then we'll have to have a look. As soon as I get a bed for you, I'll find a doctor, and we'll see what has to be done."

Within the hour, a doctor arrived who decided I should be booked for surgery when the operating room was available. "I think," he told me, "that you are trying to give birth to shrapnel, and you do have large blisters on your stump. Two or three incisions and some bed rest and you'll sit and walk comfortably. We'll have a technician check your prosthesis, the socket can't be fitting at all properly."

The doctor and nurse left while I renewed acquaintance with those in the ward. Gunner wanted to know how many loads of hay I'd taken in, No Legs surmised I must have had a row with my parents who had kicked me out, and Far Bed supposed I couldn't find a willing dame. No Arms, whose bed was now next to mine, was happy to hear my voice.

"Don't listen to those smart bastards," he exclaimed. "Just give me a hand up and tell me what the crops looked like. Was there lots of sunshine? And someone told me there was a bad thunderstorm in the Stratford area. Did you see it? What was it like?"

Gibes ignored and the blind MacKay informed, I was soon settled in. Nothing had changed except I had not seen Sister Fleda. On asking about her I was told she'd been away for two days. No Legs thought she'd be back the next morning. As before, when we had had supper, we listened to Don Messer's Islanders at 6:00, then Jim Hunter's theme "Country Gardens," and his news over CFRB at 6:30. Tired, I went off to sleep early to the music of Guy Lombardo and his band and dreamed that I was dancing gracefully with Fleda in my arms.

The next morning I was wheeled down to surgery where my needs were painlessly attended to, and I was rewarded for my good behaviour by being given two slivers of German steel that had been lodged in my backside since the long night in Holwierde when the war ended for me in the Netherlands. A day later I was able to sit without pain and had been awakened by Sister Fleda who wanted to know why I was back even as I asked her where she'd been. After I had told her of my work with Geoffrey, she explained what had happened to her.

"I had to see a doctor who ordered tests that took time —a nuisance and no report. Still we nurses must not take chances if we are to care for a young man who spends mornings jolting about on a tractor seat. Just wanted an excuse to come back to see me—right?"

Her inspection of my incisions over, she flitted away to the next bed while I watched her strong arms lift the blind Mackay with no arms to a sitting position and then manoeuvre him into his chair. Once we had all been seen to and had had breakfast, the morning's tempo slowed as we took naps or waited to see the morning's paper.

About noon I was surprised when one of the orderlies brought me a letter. It contained a notice to the effect that, on discharge from the services, I would receive a disability pension. The amount could not be divulged as the matter of war pensions was to be reviewed in the House of Commons in the near future.

Ideas of how a pension could contribute to my future ran recklessly in my mind. If I could find a desk job somewhere, this money would complement my working salary nicely. Maybe, like Betty, I could search for a comfortable apartment. A wife, too, could be a useful adjunct but with reservations if she were a star cribbage artiste. Although I was unclear as to how essential a wife was, it did occur to me as I watched Sister Fleda on her rounds that her physique and smile might compensate for her nescience of farm life. With a furnished flat in the city and years of employment behind her, she would be financially independent. Her age was a worry. I had one day asked Far Bed how old she might be.

"Oh," he replied, "she's fifty-five if she's a day for she told me she'd been a Nursing Sister in the first war. Yeah, fifty-five's about right, no doubt about it. Odd," he continued, "that she never married—must have been an inviting piece in France."

As I knew the direction of Far Bed's talk, I ended my query by saying that "whatever her age is, we're fortunate she's here." Far Bed agreed. Back on my bed I thought further about her age. She was past the child-bearing stage. If I were to marry her, we'd have to adopt if we wanted children. That course had its risks—unless, like Silas Marner, you found your Effie. For my part I tended to think adoption had its risks. The product could disappoint. On that subject I remembered the Old Man's saying: "It's breeding, Boy, that counts."

Four or five days after my arrival, a technician brought my leg back. It felt snug on me, and I was not aware of any pain from the incisions on the stump where the blisters were. The technician told me to wear it just for a few hours each day until I was ready to return home.

During that time I continued to think of the directions my future should take. I was by no means indigent. I had some savings and could look forward to employment at a desk. I did not have to marry an older woman although I found Fleda so attractive that I wanted to see more of her than I did whenever she came to my bed on her rounds. Why this was so, I couldn't tell. It was as if an aura of quiet charm circled her in the ward, a charm that led me to think of dating her, to ask her to have dinner with me before I returned to Stratford on the following Saturday. On Wednesday I gathered up my courage, when I saw her alone at the Nursing Station, and asked her if she'd like to have dinner with me on Thursday at the Royal York where she'd suggested my parents might stay.

"Oh, what a nice surprise," she answered. "Of course, I'd love it—if you can give me time to go home and change. What time would you like to leave here?"

"I have permission to be out from 6:30 on, and I could have a cab call for us here at that time so we should be at the hotel before seven."

"That's convenient for me," she said, adding "I haven't had dinner out for a long time. You are a dear boy to invite me."

Thursday passed slowly enlivened in the early afternoon by talk about pensions. McGuire and Gunner had both received the kind of pension letter I had.

"I wonder," Gunner said to the rest of us, "just how much the pension will change once it's been reviewed in Parliament."

"Don't count on being rich" was No Legs' comment. "My uncle had one from the first war, and he always complained that his full pension of $75.00 a month was dammed little compensation for being shot up and gassed."

"Did that amount never change?" Gunner asked.

"Not that I know of."

"Well," McGuire observed, "once I've bought my smokes and beer, I won't have much left for a wife will I? Our dear country isn't going to go far in debt for the likes of us."

"Seventy-five bucks is what it costs to make just one 25 pounder shell," said Gunner, adding "I wonder who's carrying the flag for us in this review?"

"I've heard a rumour," Far Bed told us, "that it's Milton Gregg who's a V.C. from the first war."

"Let's hope," I put in "that he's savvy enough to convince our politicians to add a few bucks to this dole."

"Well just remember," added No Arms, "that some assholes will argue that we asked for what we got— volunteers weren't we? Off the top of freight cars and wanting a meal when we enlisted."

"Oh horse shit!" shouted Far Bed, "I don't buy that crap."

At this point die Fleder swooped down on us saying, "Now that's enough noise and bad language. The doctor's on his way, and I don't want him to think the lot of you are beyond control. So please hush up!"

That night, walking with a cane and ignoring Far Bed's question as to where I was going, I met Fleda at the main entrance looking very different in a smartly tailored russet-coloured suit, the jacket with a single button, the skirt full and pleated. She appeared noticeably neat alongside me in my old stained serge uniform.

"Well Boy," she called to me, "you do look ready to go and regimental. Can you manage these steps?"

She did not offer to take my arm while I, anxious to show how I could manage my new leg, took the steps down one at a time till we arrived at the cab where Sister got in from the far side and I, with the driver's help, from the other side. Sister took my cane and my hand pulling me upright beside her. Directions having been given we moved off. I had never been so close to my Nursing Sister before, her thigh warm against mine and our shoulders touching. The faint fragrance from her body was more noticeable now that it was not competing with the medical odours of the ward. It was she who spoke first.

"I hope you don't mind my not wearing a hat. I did look for one when shopping the other day, but I couldn't find anything I liked. Can you imagine me in one of those saucy sailor rigs with a mess of artificial flowers on top? No, don't exercise your imagination, just accept me hatless—please."

Looking at her greying fair hair that fell in soft spirals along her neck, I said, "You don't need a hat to look pretty, Sister, although I do like to see you wearing your white veil."

Accepting my compliment, she smiled saying only, "you flatter an old lady" adding "and there's no need to call me Sister now that we are on our own—Fleda will do very nicely."

On the way to Front Street, I reached out to the soft curling fall of her hair which I told her was as fine as silk.

"Yes," she said, "I know all too well; it's the very devil to do much with."

As she threaded her fingers through mine, she told me it was not much different from hers.

"What's your mother's like?" she asked.

"Oh, I think it must be easily manageable because when I was a boy it was long, and she wore it coiled on the nape of her neck where it would remain all day long. She had it bobbed the year I went to high school."

"I had mine bobbed too, but I was such a fright that I let it grow out again. I'm certain it would never stay in place were I to try coiling it. But enough about our hair—

tell me how does your prosthesis feel now that the technician has worked on it?"

"Much more comfortable and snug and more a part of me."

"That's good," she said, "but do be careful moving into the hotel. It's a bit of a hike to the Imperial Room."

But without help I managed to get to the dining room where we both subsided into comfortably cushioned chairs at our table below one of the largest chandeliers I'd ever seen. I thought my dinner companion very attractive as she smiled across the linen with its array of gleaming silver and glass.

What I thought she revealed clearly was pleasure— not because of me, although I hoped I was part of the smile—but more likely a feeling of release from a ward of broken men into a bright world where even the waiters were, if flatteringly deferential, at least whole and nimble footed. That she was pleased, pleased me.

Her strong fingers that I knew so well had only one ornament, a gold ring with a small green stone; on her wrist was the watch I saw every day as she took my pulse. She had no necklace and no earrings. She was, as I remember her now, a plain lady without makeup whose smile, and steady blue eyes, and the natural wave of her hair more than compensated for the lack of feminine baubles. She was in a quiet way distinctive, fully aware of others but never ingratiating.

Telling the waiter we needed time to consider the menu, we did just that deciding finally to have baked flounder fillets in Marguery sauce—something I'd never had but which Fleda assured me would be good. Emboldened by my wartime savings, I told her we should have a French white to accompany the fish and a dry sherry to begin. This agreed upon and the waiter sent on his way for the sherry, we talked about ourselves. As I already knew from Far Bed that she'd served in the first world war, I asked what hospital she'd been in.

"It wasn't a hospital," she told me. "I was attached to #44 Casualty Clearing Station close to the front lines. It was often dreadful work."

As she already knew I had been a junior officer with the Perths, we spent little more time on past military activities, instead we talked about our families.

"Who," she inquired, "looked after your farm while you were in the army? Were you the only child?"

"Yes, I was the only one. My parents were alone until they found Geoffrey, a hired man who's still with them. He's in his early forties and a person that my mother says they are really fortunate to have."

"And tell me about your mother."

"Oh she looks after the house, the meals, and her flock of Barred Rocks."

Over the sherry came Fleda's next question: "Barred Rocks?"

"Hens," I enlightened her. "She always had fifty or sixty of them: the egg money is hers, and the cockerels ease the strictures of meat rationing. Mother's day is just as demanding as the Old Man's."

"And why do you call your father, the Old Man—not very polite, is it?"

"Oh, he's been the Old Man as long as I can remember, just as he's always called me the Boy, and we Geoffrey, the hired man. Perhaps he was the Old Man because he was some years older than mother with straggly hair and a bald spot. As to how I became Boy, I have no idea because my mother and my friends called me Jamie or James."

"Something else I'm curious about," she continued, "is why you're already working on the farm when you really shouldn't be. If I were your mother I wouldn't let you."

"Oh, it's something to do, a way to show my father I can be useful. Driving the Farmall was not difficult; it was Geoffrey who did the real work as we cleared out the old fence line. We have," I continued, "a reachy lot of heifers that are talented fence artists so the Old Man decided to get rid of the snake rail one and put in a galvanized one."

"Reachy heifers, fence artists, snake rail? Come again, I'm lost." Accepting my definition of the terms, as young cattle good at getting through rail fences, she kept to her question: "But why work at all? Why not laze about and watch others work? Surely your family would understand."

Fortunately the arrival of soup and then the main course freed me from explaining that on our farm no one just sat and watched others work—unless it happened to be a visiting clergyman or well-dressed city cousins in search of a good dinner. To escape further questions about our monastic existence on the 3rd Concession, I shifted away from the farm during dinner to ask about her past.

"When did you first come to Christie Street?"

"Oh just when the first wounded began arriving. Nurses were badly needed. Because of my time in France in the first war, I was seconded here from Wellesley where I'd been since 1919. I'm really an old stager you know."

"And do you like living in the city?"

"Oh, I love Toronto, it's on the move and exciting: big stores like Eaton's and Simpson's, wonderful restaurants, cinemas, and street cars to take you places. It's only quiet on Sundays. But my mother never liked it here."

"Why?"

"She was from Whitby in Yorkshire and missed the moors and the sea. After my father died and I went into nursing, she returned to Whitby where she had inherited property."

"Did you ever visit her there?"

"Oh yes, twice. She died just before the war."

"And how long were you in France?"

"Three years. I came back here just before the war ended. I was not well at the time."

Over the fish, I asked her about her name, Fleda, "rather unusual, isn't it?"

"Yes it is different," she replied. "And it really should be Enfleda which was my mother's name. Enfleda," she enlightened me, "was the name of an eighth-century abbess in Whitby, but I shortened the name because it's easier to say—and less suggestive of sanctity."

"I rather like it," I told her, "it's distinctive, and I'm sure no one here would guess its origin." She laughed as we settled in to dessert. Before coffee arrived I asked her where she lived in Toronto.

"Just off St. Clair on Oakwood. I have a small apartment—I'd like a larger place, but this one is so convenient and quiet that I keep on in it. When I need a change, I expect nice young men like James McKay to take me out to expensive restaurants."

Before I could phrase an adequate reply, our waiter appeared with coffee. Over it we had little to say as we let our sense of contentment work its charm. The bill and tip settled, we moved off to the lobby where I ordered a taxi to take us back.

On the way down I did not manage the steps as easily as I had mounted them. Aware of my uncertainty, Fleda steadied me to the taxi where a helpful driver bundled me, my cane, and the awkward leg into the back seat where I found Fleda close beside me, she having got in first. Pulling me upright she left her arm round me comfortingly as we moved off.

"I did so enjoy the dinner," she said, "especially the flounder. Wasn't the sauce for it delicious? And the dessert—so good, chocolate mousse topped with whipped cream—I shall have no appetite for anything tomorrow."

On my assuring her that I, too, had enjoyed our dinner, she reminded me I had spent a lot on the wine.

"But I liked it," she continued, "for it went so nicely with the fish and our conversation. Oh, I shall remember this dinner with you for a long, long time. Thank you Jamie."

We were seated close, my scarred face against the softness of hers. Perhaps it was the wine that encouraged me to slip my free hand under the long lapel of her jacket so that I cupped her soft breast—a move she did not dispute while we drove all too soon back to 352 Christie where, as we turned into the driveway, Fleda kissed me, saying again how much she'd liked the evening. I wanted our lips to linger, but the driver had turned for his fare while I had to tell him to take Fleda home and then get myself out of the cab and on my feet.

Back in the ward I found everyone including the inquisitive Far Bed asleep. Undressed and free of the leg, I lay in bed ignoring the phantom pains as I thought of how much I liked my World War I Nursing Sister. I wanted another date, but it would have to wait now until mid-September when I'd been told my leg would have to be looked at again to see how well I was doing on it. As Fleda was going on nights the next evening, she should, I reckoned, be back on days when I returned. Cheered by that expectation, I went off to sleep and dreamed uneasily of being wet and dirty in a slit trench somewhere beside an Italian vineyard. The morning found me dry and clean and waiting for another taxi that was to take me to Union Station and a Stratford train home.

Chapter 6

Snake Eyes

On the last day of August I was back in Stratford where I found the Old Man and mother waiting for me at the station. Greetings over, mother anxiously inquired about my week away and if I thought my prosthesis was now comfortable. I assured her it was and that the week had passed agreeably. I made no mention of my night out with Fleda thinking it unwise to set parents speculating about the expense.

"And what did they do about your backside?" the Old Man asked.

"Oh just this," as I showed him the shrapnel which the surgeon had given me.

"You had that in you!" he started. "No wonder you couldn't bear the tractor seat. Well, now that you're free of that, you can take on the fall ploughing."

"Oh for goodness sakes, John," mother cut in, "forget about your work for once. Jamie's not our hired man!"

Her retort sent the Old Man fumbling through his pockets for the Chevy's key as he set off for the car with my crutches under his arm. This time I sat in the front and mother in the back. On the drive home our talk shifted to the threshing which was nearly complete in the township where two or three farmers had combines which father maintained would eventually render threshing machines as we knew them obsolete. From the back seat mother told me that the McKay Bhard's youngest boy had broken his arm and that the young people in our church were planning their program for the fall and were looking for speakers. Talk did much to reduce the miles until the countryside became more familiar. Once back home the Old Man changed his clothes and stumped off to the cow barn to help Geoffrey pull milk from fifteen full udders while mother put on an apron and set about storing the purchases she had made earlier in Stratford.

"I did all right this morning in Loblaw's," she told me, "a rib roast of beef for 31¢ a pound and two loaves of whole wheat bread for 15¢; in the Dominion coffee was just 35¢ a pound. Such prices help reduce the grocery bill. But I do wish the government would drop the food rationing now that the war is over. I had to use up the last of my meat coupons today."

With this announcement, she disappeared into the summer kitchen to light the old three-burner coal-oil stove to heat our supper. After supper Geoffrey went off to a softball game in the village and I to the wicker chair on the verandah where I took off my leg and stump sock to let cool air in on my scarred end. Later the Old Man joined me to have his evening pipe. Mother as usual was in the kitchen clearing away and washing up at the sink.

"How did you find Stratford today?" I asked father.

"Oh pretty much as usual, a lot of returned men coming and going. I met young Daryl Bennett in the bank. I hardly knew him, he's changed so much; the skinny teen-ager is now a firm-set young man. He's still in uniform and looking for a job in town. He won't have the trouble finding work that you will."

With his blunt reminder of my missing leg, I thought it a good time to remind him that my disability was pensionable.

"How much will that amount to?" he asked.

"At present about $72.00 a month for someone with my degree of disability."

"Why do you say at present?"

"Because it may be increased; a parliamentary committee, I'm told, may be appointed soon to consider pension levels."

"Well, $72.00 a month doesn't seem to me much by way of compensating for the loss of your right leg. Had you listened to me years ago you'd have your leg now and a farm for life."

I was about to say "and wear a white feather" but refrained thinking it wise not to reopen an old wound. I knew his response: my place on the farm was essential for food production, "no need to join the Perths."

So ignoring the Old Man's challenge, I reminded him that my pensionable income would be tax free.

"But you can't live on $72.00 a month," he objected.

"I know that, but I can hold a job and still receive my pension."

"And where," he asked, "do you think you'll find work? Full-time farming, it seems to me, is out."

"I may be able," I replied, "to get a desk job in the Department of Agriculture. I do have a degree and preference may be given to disabled veterans."

"Well, good luck, Boy, you're not much use on a farm. But you can stay here until you do find something. Your mother is very pleased to have you in the house."

The Old Man left me under no illusion as to my capabilities, and it was a relief to be free of his remarks when mother joined us from the kitchen. Unlike the Old Man she was delighted to hear that my missing leg merited a pension.

"Oh, Jamie," she cried taking my hands, "how wonderful! Now you can really take your time here at home and get used to your new leg and," she added teasingly, "help me in the house."

"But," I countered, "if Mr. Drew gets the hydro down the 3rd, there'll be no work for me to do in the house."

"Oh yes there will be and, even if there's not enough, you and I can just sit, and talk, and read, and watch the men work."

"With all this idleness," said father, smiling a little, "I wonder if there'll be food on the kitchen table when I come in from work?"

"Oh I'm sure there's famine ahead for you, John— especially if you have to feed yourself—so you'd better be mighty civil to Jamie and me!"

On this note of family good humour, we all went off to bed. Later, as I lay on my bed with only a sheet over me listening to a whippoorwill somewhere in our woods, I was comfortable until a spasm of phantom pain returned to the missing leg. As I rubbed the stump I remembered how well both legs had served me on long route marches. It had been just one year before, when the Perths in battle gear left Jesi on the Adriatic to slog for two days some thirty-five miles in searing heat and dust to the edge of the Gothic Line, where in thirty-six hours I lost over half my platoon killed or wounded. And then more marching and rain, and mud, and hurt, and death. To be home and on a comfortable bed was more than a bit of all right. Relieved of memory's burden, I went off to sleep grateful that never again need I endure long route marches ending in fearsome assaults.

The next morning, feeling rested and having had a good breakfast, I was sitting in the wicker chair with yesterday's paper when I noticed two girls crossing the lawn. They came up shyly to ask me if I'd be their guest speaker at the first meeting of their young people's group. My hesitation gave way in their eagerness to engage me.

"And you can talk about anything you like Mr. McKay, and we'd like you to meet all our members and stay afterwards for coffee and doughnuts."

Once the girls had left, I spent nearly an hour puzzling

over what I should say. I dismissed battle experience as unsuited and agriculture as boring before deciding to talk about London as I'd known it on my leaves from the regiment. The subject met one of the criteria emphasized in the public speaking classes I attended at the O.A.C. where a peppery professor advised us always to go for "a personal experience." So I set about in my mind organizing an afternoon and night in London in a way that might interest local teen-agers.

That done and mother busy baking, I put on my leg and walked out to our driving shed that lay between the house and the barn. There I found Geoffrey and the Old Man removing canvases from the binder and cleaning and oiling the hayloader and tedder before putting them away until the next harvest time.

"What's your opinion of 2-4D?" father asked knowing very well he was one-up on me for I'd seen the Ag. Rep. leaving just as I'd left the house.

"I have no opinion," I told him. "I'm sure I have never heard of it. I've heard of DDT because it was used in Italy to kill mosquitoes that carried malaria. Why do you ask about 2-4D?"

"Oh, McKenzie the Ag. Rep., just told me they are experimenting with it at your College. Seems it kills weeds. All you do is spray it on growing crops. According to McKenzie it costs only a couple of dollars an acre to apply."

"Seems a bit magical," I said. "If it works you won't need that fancy scuffler you have for the corn. Odd though that it destroys weeds and spares the crop. What's it do in the soil?"

"Don't know," the Old Man replied. "Probably washes out with the rain. It'll certainly put the O.A.C. on the map if it works as they say it does."

The implements put away, Geoffrey and I went up for

dinner while father went down the lane to get the paper after which he joined us at the table. In the afternoon he went to Embro while Geoffrey scythed weeds along our fence lines, and mother picked the last of the green beans after which I heard her rattling pots and pans in the kitchen.

Then, at my post in the wicker chair, I read the paper for a time until to escape some troublesome flies, I put it over my face and dozed off to a fitful dream in which I was close up and following an artillery barrage that lit up the night on the Coriano Ridge. I was more concerned about the men in my platoon who were losing feet and legs on Schu mines than I was about the shell bursts just ahead of me. Out of breath I threw myself behind a five-foot dyke some forty miles north of Coriano along the Fosso Munio: the absurd geography of a dream! From the midst of this bifurcated nightmare, I awakened under *The Globe and Mail* to think more logically about Coriano and the Fosso Munio.

The dream gave no hint that a period of three months of fighting intervened between these two locations. No hint either of the dark waters of the Munio or of how miserably wet I was once across and dug in around some farm buildings. No reference to the artillery fire that boxed us in and repelled Germans counter attacking or to the awful cost to the Regiment: thirty-two killed and forty-nine wounded: the security for a battle honour.

It was a decided relief to jettison these cheerless memories and greet mother as she appeared with fresh tea biscuits and her own strawberry jam. Afternoon tea was by no means a tradition on our farm—it was rather an indulgence, but one I now looked for daily. Tea with my mother contributed to the easeful pattern of the warm September days when drying leaves on trees rustled rather than sighed in the breeze and wild flowers were losing their petals and revealing seeds destined for rebirth. For me the pattern was steady and comforting so unlike the ups and downs of battle along the river-laced littoral of the Adriatic. Caught up in this slow natural rhythm of our days, I was surprised to hear mother say, as she offered me a second biscuit, "Isn't it to-morrow night Jamie that you talk to our young people?"

It was, and just after seven the next day she drove me to the church. As the hall was in the basement, we could enter from the ground level without having to face stairs. Once inside, a group of pubescent young people milled about giggling and trying to mask their natural awkwardness. Among them I noticed a little boy who no doubt had badgered a sister into bringing him on the promise that he'd be good.

Once the audience was seated and I had been introduced, I proceeded to tell them what war-time London had been like especially at night in the black-out which so impressed me. My hearers seemed interested even the little boy who sat to the right just below my reading stand; he was a model of attentiveness. At the end, remembering the Guelph classroom procedure, I asked if there were any questions. For a minute or so there was silence. Taking advantage of it the little boy said something that I couldn't hear because he was on my deaf side. On asking him to move over and then speak more loudly, he did just that.

"Were you ever," he asked, "in the real war?"

On admitting that I had actually been in combat, he looked relieved and put the question that really interested him.

"Did you ever," he wanted to know, "kill a German yourself?"

As my audience waited in silence to hear the incriminating confession, I resorted to rhetorical subterfuge saying I might have, but I couldn't be sure, adding misleadingly that I hoped I had not done so. Still, my questioner was not done with me.

"How is it," he asked, "that you have a limp and use a cane? Can't you walk right?"

Answering this inquiry seemed to me less likely to lead to embarrassment, and so I told him and the others that I had an artificial leg.

"Could I see it?" the young doubter persisted.

Unwilling to risk questions as to how it happened, I thought it best to show them the whole appliance. I pulled up my trouser leg, loosened the straps and took off the leg for all to see at the same time waving my stump at my earnest questioner. It was a climactic moment as one of the girls standing to see at the back fainted and crashed over a row of empty chairs. Confusion reigned as some girls ran to the kitchen for water and others set about freeing the unconscious one from the chairs and finding a cushion for her head. She recovered quickly. I was thanked hurriedly for a most interesting talk while I reassembled my leg piece preparatory to having coffee and doughnuts with my audience.

On one hand my talk had been a crashing success; on the other, I could imagine the caustic little man, my professor, noting how minimally the climax was related to the subject itself and of how impossible it would be to grant me more than a C+ for the effort. Refreshments and the need to meet members of the audience soon put concerns about my talk to the back of my mind. I was relieved, however, when mother arrived to take me home and away from the little boy who, by the time he'd eaten his doughnut, showed signs of wanting to ask another question of me.

At home, as we moved into September's days of sunshine and cooler weather, I was pleased when my father asked me to help in the autumn's work. On the Farmall, ploughing or discing our fields, I had time to myself to remember and assess. Even the talk to the Young People's group came up for review not at all to my credit as I thought of how a child had embarrassed me, made me acutely aware of a young paratrooper's agony and pleading eyes on Ceprano's cobblestones.

And yet it was from the beginning something I myself had willed and rejoiced over: the heroic possibilities of serving my king and country "by the path of duty and self-sacrifice." But now the heroism appeared tinged with regret, almost shame, even though the killing of my enemy meant I'd survived to till in freedom the fields of my inheritance. I wondered how Fleda would respond—if she knew.

Shortly after the Labour Day week-end, the Old Man brought me a letter when he came to the house with his paper. It contained my Certificate of Service which indicated that having served in Canada, United Kingdom, the Central Mediterranean Area, and Continental Europe, I had been struck off the strength of the Canadian Army (Active). I was at last a civilian, one needing employment. What to do? Should I, as mother had suggested, seek a desk somewhere in the maze of agricultural administration? Another alternative was to use my Overseas credits to return to university for graduate work. Just one year in the Ontario College of Education and I would be qualified to teach in a secondary school. And then there was the family farm on which I appeared to be useful without the assistance of a straight-backed country girl, a willing milker.

As the Old Man's preferences were somewhat at variance with Fleda's qualifications, I decided that, in the acquisition of a wife, time was on my side. I could wait. I was smugly confident, despite my physical short comings, that I had a degree of charisma that appealed to Fleda, an attractive lady, already familiar with damaged veterans. I even thought it quite possible that she was in love with me.

By mid-September she was increasingly on my mind as I looked forward to my return to Christie Street to have my prosthesis checked and my right ear examined for hearing loss. A letter to me confirmed that my presence was required at the hospital on September 17. As before, on that day my parents drove me to the station in Stratford.

At Christie Street in late afternoon I was pleased to find Fleda on days and to hear her welcoming voice. "Well, look who's back with us, my Boy from the farm! How were things at home?"

Once I had assured her—and patients listening in— that all was well, I asked about her health.

"Oh, let's not talk about me," she said smiling, "when it's you who needs attention. Let's see your stump." I detached the leg and pulled the sock off for her inspection.

"That's much better than it was the last time," she said, "although it's a bit red on one side—better have the technician check the fit of the socket to-morrow when he's to be here. And how's your bottom? Can you drive the tractor? No pain at all? Good. And I see we have you booked in for an audiology test on Wednesday. You'll be here for a few days so make yourself comfortable, Boy."

Then she was off to see what MacKay with no legs wanted. Once he was out of bed and in his wheelchair, she attended to others, making no distinctions, treating us all light heartedly as if we were her own family. It was now the end of her day shift, and she disappeared down the ward to the nursing station where the night nurse was waiting. Then it was suppertime, the 6:30 news with Jim

Hunter, and the usual ward chatter until lights out.

The next morning, as the newspaper made its rounds, Tim McGuire informed us quietly that John McCormack had died.

"And who the hell was John McCormack?" asked Far Bed loudly enough for all to hear.

"If you weren't so ignorant a bugger you'd know," Tim retorted. "John McCormack was the finest Irish tenor I've ever heard. I cried every time I heard him sing 'Mother Machree'."

"And who wants to cry every time he hears a song?" returned Far Bed unwilling to be put down as ignorant.

"Some minds," observed McGuire, as he struggled to fold the paper with his left hand, "are so incredibly finite." Not sure of the meaning or of his rank on the scale of the incredibly finite, Far Bed signed off from the engagement he had rashly initiated. It was then we heard a thin falsetto singing coming from the blind MacKay. The words were clear and tender:

> In a field by the river my love and I did stand,
> And on my leaning shoulder she laid her
>   snow-white hand.
> She bid me take life easy, as the grass grows
>   on the weirs;
> But I was young and foolish, and now am full
>   of tears.

"I heard McCormack sing that song once," MacKay told us, "and I've never forgotten it. Another Irishman wrote the poem."

"What's it called?" Gunner inquired.

"Down by the Salley Gardens," No Arms said. "I think it's the greatest."

For a moment no one said a word, and then it was McGuire who broke the silence saying, "We've all been young and foolish, haven't we?"

The rest of the morning was commonplace. In the afternoon a young technician stopped by me to examine my leg. Noticing the redness on the stump, he said he'd have to take the prosthesis back to his shop so he could alter the fit of the socket.

"I should have it back to you in a day or so, when I'll bring you two or three new stump socks, the texture and the weave of them are the finest I've seen."

Nothing more of consequence happened until Wednesday, when going down the hall on my crutches for my audiology test, Fleda caught up to me.

"Would you mind," she said, "doing me a favour?"

"Certainly not," I told her, "if I can manage."

"I need an escort, and I'm sure you'll do nicely. Would you be willing to take me to the Royal Alex to see *Tobacco Road* this Friday? I've been given two tickets, the best in the house."

"Nothing," I replied, "could please me more than to see a play—and with you"—I added.

"Then that's done," she said, "and thank you, you're a dear boy to come with me."

"When does the play begin?" I asked.

"My tickets say 8:20."

"Is there time for us to have dinner?" I was thinking of the Royal York.

"I don't think so, in fact I'm certain there isn't. We are terribly short of nurses, and I may not get off at five. Besides I have to go home and change. No, dinner is not possible. You stay here for supper and meet me at the door about 7:30. We can have coffee or drinks after the play."

Fleda having arranged so satisfactorily the date I had hoped to make myself, I hopped off to audiology on my crutches feeling absurdly light on one foot. To see *Tobac-*

co Road at the Royal Alexandra Theatre, a play I only
knew from the newspaper notice, stirred memories of
O.A.C. when I had bit parts in student plays directed by
Scotty McLean and produced in War Memorial Hall. But
Tobacco Road at the Royal Alex with Fleda by my side:
my cup was spilling over.

And it was well my mind was taken up for the
audiology test was long and tedious. I was passed from
one person to another, asked to listen to a variety of
sounds, most of which I could not hear, and finally
directed to an ear man who emphasized that nothing could
be done for my right ear. Its drum and my right leg had
both been shattered by shell fire in Holwierde.

"You can, of course, try a hearing aid," he said, "but
I'm sure it would be a waste of money."

On this cheering note, I returned to the ward where all
the talk was of thirty-seven wounded veterans who had
just arrived in ambulances from Union Station. Extra beds
had been set up for two of them in our ward. Where the
rest of them found beds we couldn't imagine. But somewhere among Christie Street's five hundred patients space
must have been created. We saw very little of our nurses
for the rest of the day.

The next morning we heard of line-ups at our out-
patient facility. Veterans living out had to wait hours to be
seen because we were so short staffed. It was a condition
that was getting ever more noticeable. Relief would only
come, we were told, when a new hospital called Sunnybrook might open in two or three years' time. Some on
the ward had heard that eventually all long-term patients
would be transferred to Sunnybrook. The idea lacked
appeal.

"God knows," said Far Bed, "what this new place will
be like and it's to hell-and-gone way out in north Toronto.
Visitors will never find it. No thank you—I'm staying in

good old Christie."

Buoyed up by the certainty of a night out with Fleda, I was indifferent to hospital shortages and where or when Sunnybrook was to be built. Still the hours dragged by slowly enough as I fussed over how I might improve my appearance. The options were decidedly limited, but I did manage to have my serge uniform dry cleaned, the brass shone, and my hair cut. That afternoon the technician brought my leg and the new stump socks he'd promised. I could walk once more.

At 7:30 in the evening I was at the foot of our front entrance, having managed the steps easily when a taxi drove up, and I caught sight of Fleda in the back. The driver got out and bundled me, my attachment and cane in against Fleda who pulled me upright beside her. Only then was I aware she was in her "Blues": a fine navy blue serge skirt and jacket its cuffs edged with scarlet. Instead of a hat she wore a snow-white veil over her head. As the night was cool she had put over her shoulders a navy blue cape lined with scarlet.

"You do look formal—and pretty." I told her as I boldly kissed her cheek.

"Oh, I hope you like it, I haven't been out in my "Blues" for years, but tonight I did think I should strut my rank for my favourite patient."

"I've never been to the Royal Alex," I said. "What's it like?"

"Well, it's not like the Royal York. It's small and intimate and, I think, more attractive—old world-like with its marble, beautiful woodwork, and crystal chandeliers. I think you'll like it. It's made for you tonight—no steps up or down to our seats."

And once inside I was impressed, reminded at once of theatres I'd seen on leave in Rome. It was smaller but the wall coverings, the gilded plaster, the veined marble—so unlike the interior of the Imperial Room—were strangely reassuring: I'd been there before.

As we walked to our seats, Fleda did look attractive flashing scarlet and white against blue, keeping close to my left side to be free of my cane. I felt privileged to escort so noticeable a lady. Once seated, the cape folded on my lap and the cane between us, we relaxed and watched the fashions parading to seats round about us.

From the opening scene of Jeeter Lester's shack off Tobacco Road and that of his graceless son Dude throwing a ball against the loose boards of the house, we were startled by the hopeless poverty and Jeeter's favourite epithet, "By God and by Jesus." It was certainly not the kind of play that Scotty McLean would risk staging at the College. But shocking as the language and sexual needs of some of the characters were, the unrelieved grim humour, and the growing awareness of something tragic kept us firmly in our seats. After the last curtain call, we made our way on foot to a nearby nondescript restaurant for coffee and ice cream.

"I hope you weren't disappointed that I brought you to see such dreadful characters and to hear so much bad language," Fleda said, half apologetically.

"No, not at all," I assured her, "but I'm glad Tobacco Road is in Georgia and not just outside Toronto. And I wonder how you felt about the characters. Were you as caught up in the misery of their lives as I was?"

"Oh yes! And you do feel sorry for them—which is, I suppose, an indication of just how good the acting was."

"You're right," I said. "And it's the sort of acting I'm not likely ever to see in Stratford, so I hope the next time I'm your patient, you'll let me take you to an early dinner and then to the Royal Alex—promise?"

"Oh I'd love that with you. Even *Tobacco Road* brightens existence and detours the mind." There was a pause and Fleda continued. "This has been a very special night for me, one I want to remember."

"Why so special?" I inquired.

"Because Boy, today was my last day of work at Christie Street, and I was able to have you for my escort for the night out. I hope you did not mind too much taking care of a World War I Nursing Sister."

Mimicking Jeeter, I replied that "By God and by Jesus" I was honoured and that I very much hoped we'd be together again soon.

"I, too," she said, "if it's possible."

Before I could ask the reason for the "if," the taxi I'd summoned arrived. Fleda got in first to help me from within. This time, with the driver's assistance, I was three-quarters in when the boot part of my leg caught against the edge of the car door sending me down on my side on the back seat where Fleda's strong arms pulled me over to her until my head was on her lap.

"Now I've got you," she whispered.

I made no effort to sit up nor did she offer to help me. Instead as I turned on my back, she cupped my face in her hands letting the scarlet lining of her cape screen us. Keeping her voice low by my left ear, I heard her say:

"I'm going to miss you when you go back to the farm and your mother. Do you think you'll miss me?"

"Of course, I will," I replied, "I like you."

"Always," she persisted.

"Always, and forever—if you'll kiss me."

"You are my very own Boy," she said as she kissed my lips and retrieved a wandering hand.

What remains with me still is the warmth of that kiss which I took as greedily as a baby anxious for its mother's nipple and how much I regretted the brevity of this touch of lips. We did not talk during the few minutes left—just held one another close in our cramped quarters—her fingers playing over my face as if seeking some identity, some assurance much as I'd seen the blind MacKay do with his elbow ends.

As the taxi arrived at 352 Christie, Fleda told the driver to wait while she accompanied me up the steps telling me I had helped put a dramatic end to her working career. With my departure already arranged for in the morning and fearing to lose so amiable a companion, I asked if I might come to see her in Toronto later on. Almost at once she became the die Fleder of the night shift—remote and professional.

"No Boy, you must not pursue me, it would not be at all prudent. I've been, I'm afraid, too reckless, too encouraging to-night."

"But why?" I asked bewildered by her sudden propriety.

"Good reasons, Jamie."

"And what are they?" I demanded.

"To begin," she replied, "you would be missing much if you got tangled in the apron strings of an old Nursing Sister who once threw for a seven and turned up snake eyes."

"What do you mean snake eyes?"

"No use asking Jamie, the game played out long ago in another war."

"But today is not long ago," I protested.

"No James, it isn't, and I could almost wish it were. I am, I must tell you far from well. My own doctor has told me I may have only weeks left—to live. It's a cancer that's metastatic and moving fast."

"I'm sorry," I stammered. "I'll come to see you if you'll let me." Taking my hand and giving me the lightest of kisses, Fleda said firmly:

"No, James, I could not possibly bear it. Tonight we've come to port and to part. You're a dear boy whom

I like more than I should—more than I'm entitled to—and I'm shamelessly grateful. But now it's farewell—and forever." Then she flitted noiselessly down the stone steps to a cab's empty paradise, and I never saw her again.

Of course I was disappointed, even dismayed as I thought of how rewarding the future had seemed. Later on, however, I had to admit that this brief infatuation was perhaps as much my doing as Fleda's. And not at all to my credit as I considered what I wanted: sympathy and someone to immolate herself in the care of a young man, deaf on one side, with a halting gate, an ugly scarred face, and an extremely uncertain future. Had the Old Man known of this evening encounter he would, I'm certain, have sided with Fleda.

"Good common sense," he'd pronounce as he'd clear his pipe of ash on the verandah rail. "No good ever came of messing around with an old woman. Find yourself a strong country-bred girl with a straight back . . ."

He'd have no need to expand the familiar outline of the country-bred girl. But such rural common sense, as I remembered his advice, did nothing to abate my disappointment. I wanted Fleda and could not accept the finality of her departure. Unhappy and cosseting a secret I could not share, I boarded the train on Saturday that would return me to an uncertain future on our family farm.

Chapter 7

An Ending

"What I'll never be able to understand," the Old Man remarked more to himself than to me, "is how our Rob could give up a safe and needed place on our farm to risk his life with the Perths. That Sam Hughes and his propaganda machine have much to answer for. If Rob had stayed with me, I could have farmed the two hundred acres at Kemptville. Without him, it was too much so we sold out and moved here. Rob was a true black McKay," he went on, "not fair like you and better than you with cattle and tools."

"How was it," I asked, "that he chose the Perths?"

"Oh, his friend was from Stratford and talked Rob into joining that regiment.

"You're not complaining about Rob again are you?" It was mother joining us from the kitchen where her acute hearing seldom missed the thread of conversations on the verandah when the house door was open to the screen door.

"Well," the Old Man said, "I was only telling the Boy how well we'd have done if Rob had not been so daft as to enlist when he was needed on the farm."

"Now John we've been over all that before, and it's no use your talking that way about Rob—and well you know it."

To quiet what threatened to be a parental tumult, I shifted away from Rob's enlistment to ask father if Rob had ever written to him after he'd joined up.

"Oh I had three or four letters, but there was very little

in them; he was not a letter writer. I've forgotten what he said except in the last one he told me he'd been wounded and was in a convalescent camp. Then we got the official word that he'd been killed. And now," he went on, looking at me, "we've got you without a leg and deaf in one ear—thanks to another war that's left you helpless."

"What do you mean helpless?" mother asked. "Really I could kick you John. Who's been ploughing for you? Just you be thankful Jamie's here. And he's not helpless at all."

"Yes, yes, I know," the Old Man answered, "but look at him. He can't even shift a bag of wheat into a hopper or build a load of hay."

"Well he can't help it, can he?" Mother chimed in defensively.

"I suppose not, but it was a war three thousand miles away. Had he stayed with me when he was needed . . ." the Old Man's voice trailed off as mother spoke.

"Now let's give over this but-and-if talk—it's mean of you John. Jamie can look after himself, and, despite what you say, he's been a great help in the house where I hope he'll stay as long as he likes—even if he can't shift a bag of your wheat."

I said nothing while the domestic storm eased off and the quiet of the October evening filtered around us. Mother and father had me on the family scales and had weighed me according to their measures. In going away to lead an infantry platoon in battle, I had made myself unfit to be an active farmer.

Not at all easy to defend the choice I made in 1940 as I remembered how in July of that year I had received my Bachelor of Science in Agriculture from the aged Sir William Mulock and had come home an able-bodied man. Along with my degree, however, I held a more ominous credential, my Canadian Officers Training Corps Certificate "A" in the infantry that made me eligible for consideration for a commission in the Active Militia of Canada.

For the consideration offered by that Certificate, I set aside the practice of agriculture for four years. And yet what was the call—as the Old Man put it—that justified my enlisting in an enterprise that might well demand my life as it had in another war my Uncle Robert's? Was it just an abstract ideal blotting out my father's good common sense or was it a desire not to be found missing from the ranks of my fellow Aggies: young men rallying in defense of a mother country they'd never seen and whose mistreatment of many of their ancestors accounted for their being Canadians? And why was I now quite unprepared to admit I'd made a mistake? Instead, it was an experience I was proud of, even cherished, when I could set aside the young paratrooper's face and eyes and blood.

My silence ended abruptly as my mother, hoping to end the Old Man's recitation of the wrong done to him by a brother and a son, put down her knitting saying she had to see to the stew she was preparing for the next day's dinner. Father, too, got up to raid the bicarbonate of soda to ease his stomach no doubt churning over his family's bad wartime decisions.

Left on the verandah, as darkness began seeping about the lawn's shubbery and across our fields, I gave up trying to defend a past decision that had taken me to the patterned hell of the hills and river beds of the Gothic Line. It was less trying to consider the long move from Italy to France and on to Kemmel in Belgium—almost a holiday tour. It was in Kemmel that the Perths first saw action in 1915. There we stayed for three weeks, and I was able to visit Uncle Robert's grave.

All too soon we were in action again crossing the Netherlands from Nijmegen to the Zuider Zee and east into the Province of Groningen where in the pretty village of Holwierde my active life as a soldier ended just eleven days before we received the cease-fire order. My platoon was the leading unit that at nightfall on April 23, 1945 crossed through Able Company into Holwierde. The platoon was followed by the rest of Baker Company under the command of the Major, whom we all knew as "Bomber" Chamberlain. As we moved up to the little river that divided the village, we found Germans on the other side waiting for us. They had already blown up the bridge across the river.

It's impossible to exaggerate what we endured that night as machine gun bursts from across the river and heavy artillery fire from Delfzijl forced us to hunker down in the rooms and basements of Dutch houses while we listened to continuous explosions of air burst shells, to falling walls, and showers of roof tiles clattering down on the streets. Burning houses gave a kind of eerie visibility as we peered out toward the enemy. The call for stretcher bearers was ever constant as the air bursts penetrated our hiding places. To find how others of my platoon were faring in a house across the street, I raced over some time before dawn to find that one of my best men, Kesselring, was badly hurt. And that's all I remember of my night in Holwierde or of Kesselring who had always maintained he was a relative of Albert Kesselring who commanded the German forces in Italy. What actually happened to me only became clear as I moved from one medical unit to another far from battle.

"And why are you sitting out here alone in the dark?" It was my mother, who having seen to the stew and set dishes out for the morning, was joining me on our verandah.

"What were you thinking about?" she continued.

"Oh, the end of my soldiering in a little village in

Holland."

"Was that where you were wounded?"

"Yes, and I wasn't the only one; I heard months later that the Perths lost in that one night twenty-three lads wounded and eight killed. It was an awful night."

"And what happened after you were wounded?"

"I simply can't remember—whether it was shock or morphine—I can't tell. Only later in Bielen, where my leg was amputated, was I conscious enough to realize how badly I'd been hurt."

"Well, you've certainly been through a lot," mother said, "and here you are back with old folks on a farm in West Zorra where there's no excitement, too much hard work, and too little by way of return—surely a let-down?"

"Perhaps," I replied, "but peace is quiet and subdued; war loud and monstrous—so I'm not at all prepared to complain about life on our Concession. Wasn't it you who used to say that we receive but what we give?"

"Yes, I know, and I still believe it, although on this farm we have to give rather too much for what we receive."

"Do you ever think," I asked, "your having given up a career as a teacher to become a farmer's wife and have a baby was a sacrifice?"

"No Jamie, never—you were a wonderful reward. From the time I"—mother paused and rephrased—"from the time you were but a baby, I found you endlessly re-warding, and you are still so, even though you did leave me to go to war."

"Well, there's absolutely no chance of my ever doing that again," I reassured her, "and maybe I can help the Old Man make the farm pay more than it has been."

"With you home again, I think it already is a richer place—and just look," she exclaimed, "at that big lovely orange moon peeking over the rim of our world, how I'd love to hold it in my arms!"

We sat silent for some time just looking and then, with my mother's hand at my elbow, we made our way to a night's rest. In my bed, the mindless turmoil of battle, the old Man's worries, and the phantom pains in my missing part all eased away as I watched the autumn moon lose colour and size and slip beyond the outline of my window. Sleep put an end to the mind's tangled confusion.

The next morning, when we finished breakfast, mother told father and me to wait as she wanted approval for an order she was making out from Eaton's new fall and winter *Catalogue*. Clearing a space on the table, she put the *Catalogue* down with an order sheet beside it. The Old Man made no objections to the items she'd already chosen: a galvanized pail at 95¢, Eaton's Mayfair soap five cakes for 25¢, five yards of white cotton Terry towelling for $1.60, and a stable fork with four tines for $1.05. To the list father asked her to add a garden spade with a D-handle also priced at $1.05. It was when mother mentioned adding to the list a brown wool worsted man's suit at $23.50 that, raising his eyes, father asked testily, "and who needs that?"

"You do!" mother retorted. "If you think I'm going any more to church with you when any woman can see I've mended the seat of your pants and can see, when you put your collection on the plate, how threadbare the cuffs of your jacket are"—here she paused before adding the sacrificial clincher—"and I'm doing without a new fall coat for Jamie's mink fur—and a hat—so I won't be ashamed of your clothing."

Dismayed by the vigour of his wife's assault that touched not only upon his appearance and pocket book but also his pride, father told her brusquely that he'd think about a new suit and let her know before noon. From past encounters of this sort, mother knew that the Old Man had already agreed to the purchase, but I decided it might be wise to apply a bit more persuasion by saying that I shared my mother's concern.

"If you'll agree to the purchase of a new suit," I said, "I'll buy mother the fall coat and hat as part payment for the very good meals I'm having every day in this house."

"No need to do that," father growled, "if she really needs new clothes, I can afford them."

"No, no," I told him; "this is something I want to do for my mother—and I insist—so let's have no more talk about necessity."

"All right then," the Old Man mumbled, "have it your own way," and turning to mother he said, "you can order the suit for me."

That said, he got up from the table, took his denim jacket from the door and set off in search of Geoffrey. It was not difficult for mother to choose the coat she wanted as she'd already looked carefully at the pictures in the *Catalogue*. I quite approved her selection: a light grey herring bone tweed cut wide enough to slip over a suit and with a warm lining and chamois to the waist. To go with it she chose a Lady Biltmore pancake-type beret.

"Are you sure," she asked, "that you want to spend all this money on me? Coat and hat will add up to $35.00. Why not let me use the egg money I've saved? I'm getting 45¢ a dozen for my Grade A's. And you've already given me the lovely mink scarf."

"No," I insisted, "you are to have the coat and hat, too, and no talk about using egg money."

"Well you are really much too generous, and I don't know how I can repay you. Chocolate cakes and cinnamon rolls won't begin to do it," she said, as she toted up the cost of the order and put it in the envelope that Eaton's supplied, telling me that she'd get a postal money order in Embro in the afternoon and mail off the order.

For the next two hours I manned the Acme washer and wringer while mother sorted and rinsed and put the laundry out on the line to dry under a warm sun. After that with coffee and cinnamon rolls we sat on the sunny side of the verandah where, after inquiries as to how well I'd slept and apologies for her husband's moody temper, she offered her own explanation.

"He does have his worries, you know. Before breakfast this morning he told me Geoffrey may be leaving us in November. It seems a friend of his in the village, who works in town, can get a job for him as a night watchman in a factory where he can make $200.00 a month for working five nights a week. What he makes here, thirty-five dollars a month including his room and board for working six days a week and milking on Sundays is, he says, not nearly enough at his age when he needs to save money. And we on the farm can simply not afford to pay him anymore than we are."

"So what," I asked, "will father do when Geoffrey leaves?"

"Goodness knows, probably try to get the Logan boy for the milking. Farm help since the war is as scarce as twenty dollar bills. But—she went on—let's not spoil our coffee time by worrying, John does enough of that for both of us, and do put butter on your roll."

"And how," I asked a little later, "is your arthritis behaving?"

"Oh, it's always bothersome. Yesterday I smashed one of our wedding presents, a Worcester cup and saucer. I shouldn't have got it out, but I wanted to dust the china cabinet. I simply cannot trust my hands anymore—see how these fingers are curling and feel the hard lumps at the edge of my palms."

"They are bad," I said. "Can anything be done for the

fingers?"

"No, not a thing—I just have to put up with them and hope they don't get worse."

"And what about father?" I continued, "Does he have any arthritis?"

"No, not a bit, but Jamie I do worry about his stomach and chest pains. He's not sleeping well, and three times in the past month I've found him downstairs in his chair in the night. He says that, when his indigestion is bad, he's more comfortable sitting than lying."

"Well, we were going to make an appointment. Let's do it. You told me the other day you knew a Dr. Currie in Stratford."

"Yes, but I don't know him well. I saw him when I was having my varicose veins attended to—and I rather liked him."

"Then why don't I telephone him right now while we're alone here?"

On mother agreeing to my proposal, I was in a few minutes talking to the doctor's receptionist who told me Dr. Currie was on holidays. "Could I help you?" she inquired.

I described our need whereupon she said she could arrange a date but not until November 7. This I accepted and told mother who had set about getting dinner. The noon meal passed without reference to my inadequacies or to the order for the new suit. Supper talk revealed that the outside work had gone well. By evening Geoffrey was off to pitch one of the last games of the season.

Alone for a while in my wicker chair as the day's light weakened, I began wondering about Fleda and her health. I had not thought much about her in the midst of our farm activities. But on two occasions she was memorably in mind. The first was one Sunday in church when our minister's sermon on Lazarus detoured to Mary and

Martha. We were even pointedly asked if we ourselves had known friends like these sisters. Well behaved as we were, no one offered any evidence to support such knowledge. I might have ignored his question completely but just ahead of our pew was the Logan family and playful Betty in a pretty cotton plaid dress, the red of which matched her unruly red hair. From then on I gave up on the symbolic significance of Lazarus' return to life and privately began to relate our minister's question to Betty and Fleda who might, I thought, serve as Martha and Mary.

But the comparison fell apart, although I thought Fleda could stand without challenge as a Mary. Betty, however, simply failed the test. After the service, while we stood outside talking to the Logans, Betty asked me with laughter in her eyes if I weren't game for another round of cribbage. She'd be home until Monday noon if I'd come over. Not willing to risk another round of skunks and knowing that on Monday morning I'd be needed to help mother on the Acme at home, I said it was most unlikely I'd be free. That Betty would be free on a Monday morning to play cribbage simply made her, I thought, a dubious parallel for St. Luke's much cumbered Martha.

The second occasion was entirely visionary. In a dream I saw both Betty and Fleda drift down the moonlight through my window to stand invitingly at my bed's foot. Their diaphanous negligees revealed seductively the contours of their bodies. Fleda seemed uneasy more shadowy than Betty whose smile was as inviting as her breasts. Free of restraint and disguise, Betty so captivated me that I squeezed over in my bed to welcome her to my arms. That hospitable gesture awakened me to spasms of phantom pains and the loss of my diaphanous visitors.

Awake, I lay for some time thinking of how dreams

tease and tempt our flesh obliterating operative reason. Further thought gave credence to the dream's suggestiveness. Bedding down with Betty would, I was sure, at any time ensure frisking and passion below the covers.

But it was Fleda, the one I might never have, whom I wanted. It was she, not Betty, who hovered over my mind's edge in quiet moments. It was her body that held me captive. Such desires on my part were, I knew, as unreal as my dreams. Neither Betty nor Fleda was ever likely to share my bed or milk Holsteins for me.

Because the tractor was not needed on the land for the rest of the week, I spent most of my time in the house helping mother who was pleased when I insisted on peeling potatoes, a chore that pained her hands. Over cups of tea or coffee, I came to see her as I had not done in the past. Unlike her husband, she resisted the subjugation of mind and body on the farm to financial gain.

"What's the use," she'd exclaim, "of working from dawn to dark and saving every penny for your old age when you cannot be at all sure of having it? Your father's idea of getting ahead and caring for pennies takes away the little delights living can offer. Those delights can ease the bumps on the road that all of us take for a few short years. And some bumps," she said, looking at me over her cup of tea, "mark you for life. All the more reason then to seek a little happiness before the bloom is shed."

Within our house it was the Viking radio that often served up little delights to relieve the monotony of labour and the tensions emanating from the Old Man. After the noon meal mother sat to hear the Happy Gang; in the evenings all of us waited for Don Messer and his PEI music makers before hearing Jim Hunter's "Country Gardens" and the news. Even the Old Man relaxed and laughed at Charlie McCarthy and Fibber McGee. We owed much to the magic of the air waves.

By the first of the next week I had taken up a share of the work outside as I sat cushioned on the Farmall ploughing fields along our concession. At the same time Geoffrey with the Percherons was doing the same work on the Logan acres. I even had father's approval at the end of the day to ladle out a meal mixture to the cattle and oats to the Percherons before they were turned out to the pasture. It was all rather trivial—the sort of chore I was given as a boy—but satisfying for I was being useful, as father understood the term.

And so the misty days of Indian summer enlivened by flaming autumn colours lulled us all into setting aside November's chill and damp. The Old Man was quiet, concerned I'm sure, about how he was ever going to manage when capable Geoffrey was no longer with him. The one stimulant that roused him to speech existed in the news items he found in *The Globe and Mail* at the end of his dinner. Addressing mother and me over the noon table we'd hear from behind the paper:

"Now this really puts that rascal Jolliffe in his place!" Waving a page of the paper, he'd go on to announce, "The Le Bel Commission has made its report and our Mr. Drew is completely exonerated. All that damned nonsense and legal costs over this Gestapo issue! But what can you expect from a fellow like Jolliffe, a Socialist? And it's a shame that Churchill lost to Attlee, another Socialist. Let's just hope we never have to be governed by that tribe!" A day or so later he was equally heated about the national budgetary deficit of $2,150,000,000.

"Quite beyond my comprehension—we'll be generations paying it off." Pausing and returning to my own role in this budgetary disaster he continued:

"And that's what comes in the end of going off to war, to say nothing of thousands of good men lying forever underground or of those who come home unable to do a hard day's work." Replying to mother's question of how he'd like to be under the thumb of one of Hitler's deputies, the Old Man dismissed the possibility brusquely:

"Hitler was Europe's responsibility—not ours. We had no business rushing off at once to rescue poor old England—as if we had not shed enough blood for her just thirty years before. When are we ever going to learn to look after our own acres?"

A few days later, when Geoffrey was already on his way to the stables, the Old Man grew even more heated as he turned to the paper's account of the Windsor strike.

"Here we are," he shouted, "in West Zorra not even able to hire a farm hand when there are hundreds of men standing idle on Windsor streets waiting for Ford Motors to give them more pay and shorter working hours. And this has been going on now for more than two months. Where's it to end? I'll tell you. Give those placard-carrying idlers more money and I, John McKay, will have to pay more for the next car or tractor I buy. And nobody, I'm damned sure, is going to give me more money for a hundred of milk. And that Geoffrey should use some common sense or he'll be carrying a placard on a Stratford street corner."

"All right, all right!" mother interrupted, "before prices go up, I suggest you calm down and get out of my kitchen so that I can get on with my work."

Muttering to himself, the Old Man rose and moved off to get his sweater and jacket. I watched as he put them on and then was surprised to see him wince and stumble a bit as he reached for the door. Mother, too, saw his uncertain footing as he left.

"You'd better follow him," she said, "and see what he's doing. He may not be well."

A few minutes later I found him and Geoffrey on the

barn floor taking the racks off the hay wagon so that the box could be used to hold turnips once they had been pulled and topped. Geoffrey had hold of one end of a rack and the Old Man the other. To free the heavy elm rack from the steel loops that held it securely, both men had to lift upwards. Straining, they freed it and stood it by the side of the hay mow.

It was then I noticed the Old Man looking bewildered and trying to undo the buttons on his jacket as if he wanted to reach inside. At the same time his face twisted and his knees buckled and rather like the young man I'd shot in Ceprano, he sank down looking imploringly on me for explanation. I sent Geoffrey off on the run to the house to tell mother to call the hospital's emergency number while I did what I could to make my father comfortable. I loosened his shirt collar for his breathing was in gasps. His lower lip was twisted downwards, and his eyes seemed no more to see me.

Geoffrey returned as quickly as he left. Breathless, he said a hospital doctor had told mother to get her husband to the hospital as fast as she could. At the same time I saw her backing the Chevy out of the garage and heading for the barn. Once at the barn doors, mother helped Geoffrey get the Old Man into the back seat where she had tossed pillows and a blanket. With her at the wheel we were at Emergency in less than an hour. There, attendants disappeared with her husband on a trolley still struggling for breath.

An hour later an intern came to us. "Your husband," he told mother, "is dangerously ill. He's had an ischemic stroke, and his right side is paralysed." It would be better —he advised her—if she waited until later to see him."

Mother decided to stay at the hospital while Geoffrey and I returned to look after livestock and the chores. Later in the evening we drove back to the Stratford General.

Mother took us in to see the Old Man. He seemed asleep behind the oxygen mask and unaware of mother as she took his hand and kissed his forehead. An hour later we left and drove mother home.

Over cups of coffee that night she gave way to emotion as she talked of how little chance the doctors held out for her husband's recovery. "Oh Jamie," she said wiping away tears, "he was just a farmer, but he was my man and good to me. I shall so miss him if he dies." On my reassuring her that I'd stay by her and do all I could to help on the farm, she said she'd call Jenny Logan in the morning to find out if her son Lorne could work for us. Afterwards we said goodnight and moved off sadly to our beds.

For another four days we ran a shuttle service to the hospital. Throughout our vigils the Old Man from time to time seemed to know us as he held out his left hand to take ours. We could make nothing of his speech, a guttural gargle. Sometimes I thought I could hear the word Boy, but that may have been my imagining. Frustration made him slap his left hand on the bed while tears coursed down the creases on his weathered face. Then, giving way to the euphoria of morphine, his eyes would close, and he'd seem asleep.

Early on the morning of the fifth day, on answering a telephone call from the hospital, mother was told her husband had died peacefully. An hour later we saw the body, the face an ashen shade, his strong hands pale and limp, his face drawn over on the right side. Later on we went to Goody and Bustin's Funeral Home where a suave gentleman in a pin-striped suit greeted us sympathetically, asked about our wishes for the preparation of the body, and the kind of service we'd like. Finally, in reply to mother's question about costs, he took us to an upper display room to show his range of caskets from polished oak with rich interiors and gold handles to plain grey ones with brass handles.

Goody and Bustin's did all it could to give death a kind of status, to hush up its grief, to make us feel somehow privileged in the quiet of its deeply carpeted floors, discreet lighting, and the functioning of its forced air heating that washed a slightly perfumed warmth over us. Not at all the service we gave our dead in Italy's testing weather. I thought Goody and Bustin's management of man's final end deserved some credit although mother's remark on the way home suggested it was far from being a charitable enterprise:

"Four thousand dollars seems awfully expensive to me, Jamie. Isn't your father ending up a spectacle for profit?"

Thinking of our neighbours and of how even the poorest of them would want to appear decently clothed and housed for their exit—and to allay mother's disquiet about the cost—I replied, "As he was my father I'd not like to think I'd failed him in any way at the end. He expected much of me, and I disappointed him. For my part I want him to be well remembered."

"I understand Jamie . . . it's mean of me to worry about costs, but $4000.00 will eat up most of his savings."

"Oh I know it's a lot of money, but it's father's, and we should use it. He'd like a bit of show. So don't worry about it. He worked hard for his place in the sun."

"You're right there Jamie, but I do wish he'd had a bit more ease and fun during his time with us and less show at the end."

"Well, we all make choices for better or worse, don't we?" I observed, as we turned into our lane where we saw Geoffrey and Lorne Logan bringing the cows into the barn.

"Oh I do hope," mother said, "that Lorne can work for us. He wasn't sure when I telephoned before we left for

Stratford this morning. It's too much to expect Geoffrey to do all the milking. He's been getting up at four in the morning so as to have it done on time for pick-up. But Lorne must have decided. We'll certainly need him when Geoffrey leaves us."

At the house we discovered that the mail man, an old acquaintance, had left a large parcel no doubt thinking it would be safer there than on the road; it was our Eaton's order. As it was nearing suppertime, we decided to leave off opening it until later. Getting the evening meal ready was made easy when Jenny Logan and Mrs. McKay Bhard came to the door bearing supper dishes for us. A choice made and the men in, mother asked the Logan boy if he'd be able to work for us.

"Oh yes, Mrs. McKay, but for the next three or four days only for the milking as I have to shingle the garage at home."

"And that will suit us very nicely, won't it Geoffrey?" Geoffrey's nod of agreement, as he filled his mouth with a slice of donated lemon pie, indicated his agreement.

Supper over, mother and I washed up, cleared the table and opened the parcel. There for our inspection were all the items we had ordered including the Old Man's suit and mother's fall coat which had all the features the *Catalogue* had listed down to the two deep slashed pockets. As she tried it and the beret on, I asked her to find her mink scarf. This done and the scarf in place, I thought she looked smart, not at all like a plain Zorra housewife. Smiling she put her arms round me and kissed me saying, "Oh Jamie you've been so good to me—if only John were here to see me—thank you so much." Almost at once her quick mind was a day ahead as she announced: "We must go into Stratford first thing in the morning to Goody and Bustin's because I want John to be laid out in his new suit—you'll come with me, won't you?"

"Of course, and we can find out what arrangements have been made for the wakes."

More talk followed, as we cleared away the cartons and wrapping, checked to see that we'd received all the items we'd been billed for, and wisely, decided to retire early.

Chapter 8

Not My Child

His obituary in *The Stratford Beacon-Herald*, which my mother and I had prepared, seemed adequate:

> Suddenly after a brief illness at the Stratford General Hospital on Monday, November 12, 1945 in his seventy-second year John McKay of the 3rd Concession, West Zorra. Beloved husband of Jean Andrews, father of James. Pre-deceased by his brother, Robert.

The rest of the notice was the familiar routine for services as promoted by Goody and Bustin's.

Of course, something more could have been said. But it was hardly necessary, for I was really surprised by the numbers who came to pay their respects at the funeral home. The place resembled a rained-out family picnic that had reconstituted itself indoors. Amid the hot-house sweetness of cut flowers and the odour of Pond and Revlon products, country women hatted and suitably serious, stood with their men whose calloused hands seemed ill at ease at the end of the sleeves of their Sunday suits. Shyly they moved toward us to tender their sympathy—sometimes with tears—as they viewed my father splendid in his new brown worsted from Eaton's.

For two evenings at Goody and Bustin's, my mother bore up well meeting all the expectations of the wakers by giving her hand with its arthritic fingers, her smile of recognition, and her thanks for their sympathy. Then she

99

took them one by one or in pairs to the coffin flanked with flowers where they could look their last on their neighbour. He looked, I thought, as if he'd recovered from his stroke and was magically asleep. The twisted side of his face and lower lip had been surgically restored and partially concealed in a fold of satin.

"He does look so nice and natural, doesn't he?" was as frequently spoken as the more discerning, "I'm sure we'll all miss him as you will Jean."

Convention in the funeral home had tidied death's messiness into the acceptable supported by respectful gestures and phrases long minted in rural consciousness. In reminding us so comfortably and starkly of our own ends, Goody and Bustin's justified without obvious personal intrusion its own financial success.

Because I had managed to get an appointment with a Stratford dentist some two weeks before, I was able to see a Dr. Searle on Wednesday morning. He examined my partial plate, smoothed off surfaces that were irritating my lower gum and advised me to arrange through the Army to have a new plate made. Until then I'd have to put up with mealtime clicking—an audible reminder of a failed attack across the Riccio.

The wakings over that evening, the funeral and interment in the Presbyterian cemetery followed the next day. Again I was surprised by the number of mourners, many of whom gathered afterwards in our home to eat from the plates of sandwiches, cookies, and cakes which they had contributed. The formalities of waking, church attendance, and graveside procedure behind them, the neighbours were more relaxed and reverted in talk to what they knew best: their friends, their livestock, and the weather.

Jenny Logan took on the duty of hostess for mother, seeing to it that no one's hand was long without food. She told me Betty could not come to the funeral as she now had a part time job in Woodstock. Her father, Charles, spoke later on to me saying he was pleased we could make use of Lorne. I was not to worry about the lease, he said, for we could discuss that at a later date.

Joe Callan, whose farm was two concessions west of ours, reminded me of the latest Toronto happening, the laying of the cornerstone for the Sunnybrook Memorial Hospital.

"I suppose," he said, "you'll look forward to going there. When it's complete, it will be really up-to-date. Christie Street," he went on, "was all right in my time, but that was thirty years ago."

Joe, I knew, had been wounded in the Great War about the same time my Uncle Robert had been killed. Joe recovered fully after months in hospitals in England and in Christie Street. Like the Old Man, he was a good farmer. I was not, however, prepared to admit that medical care at Sunnybrook would make me disloyal to Christie Street.

"Christie," I informed Joe, "still has much to recommend it, and the nursing care is excellent."

Before I could say more in defence of Christie's services, a neighbour interrupted and took Joe off to one side leaving me thinking of Fleda and her health. As others came up to speak to me, she remained on my mind an uneasy image threading its way in and out of my consciousness like some bird of the night. I had tried to get in touch with her when in Stratford by telephoning Christie Street and getting her telephone number. I called her three or four times and got no answer.

As the November sun slanted to the west and into the nearby bare tops of the maples, it was apparent, as food and talk diminished, that we must have appeased the Old Man's tutelary deities. Men began freeing their wives from last minute bits of social chatter to say goodbye to mother so that they could return to overalls, smocks, and work boots at home where cattle stood to be milked, fed, and bedded. Chores had to be done whatever the occasion. And now that a neighbour had been fittingly celebrated and returned to the good earth that he had tilled so well and long, there was no excuse to linger with the women.

At last my mother and I were left alone sitting in the Old Man's study. Her staying power, her acceptance of rural well meaning, her calm deportment, her frailty—so obvious now when she tried to rise from a chair—drew my sympathy. It was as if I recognized a person other than the one who had comforted me in hurt or illness, guided me in school work, and served as a barrier between me and my father's driving energy. Impossible not to admire her as she sat quietly having witnessed how life in the end deals with all of us. Unlike Uncle Robert, her John would have no proud scroll under a royal coat of arms to commemorate a lifetime of triumphing over soil, and yet he, too, "had passed out of the sight of men." For a time we were silent, she sitting near me rubbing her hands gently in her lap and I, having removed my leg, rubbing my stump to ease the pain either from standing too much or from a socket that no longer fitted as it should. She spoke first.

"My hands really ache to-night. They feel as if they were on fire. Too much hand shaking. Some men grab your hand as if they were taking up a shovel. Feel them, Jamie."

I took both her hands in mine and then, without warning, began to cry. It was embarrassing. I was a little boy again feeling sorry for myself wanting sympathy from a woman who had seen Death and stared him down with courage. As she withdrew her hands and rose wincing from her chair, mother exclaimed, "Oh Jamie, this won't do at all."

As I wiped my eyes and recovered my composure, she moved toward the roll-top desk saying, "I'm going to get you a drink, and I shall have one, too." From a small drawer on the left of the desk, she took a key which opened a bottom drawer from which she took a full bottle of Islay Scotch whisky.

"Your father always kept a bottle just in case, he said, of a real emergency—and it had to be real, almost fatal, before he'd get the key to the Islay. Tonight's emergency is special, and it seems to me to justify a dram without excuse."

From the dining room she brought tumblers and from the kitchen a small pitcher of water. She asked me to pour the drinks, afraid lest she'd drop her husband's rarely taken medical nostrum. Seated, she looked at me and said, "Now let's be firm—no more tears." Then, to my surprise raised her glass and said clearly, "Here's to John McKay, my good friend for thirty years—may he rest in peace." We touched glasses, said his name, and drank to the Old Man we'd known so well.

Later, as the whisky worked its charm and the evening sun spread a veil of saffron along the horizon, we talked about the husband and father, now a memory only.

"Strange," I said, "how we fall into a sense of permanence on the farm, that like the seasons we'll just go on and on. Death always seems a surprise. No one's ready to accept it."

"But," mother responded, "we've been warned many times that we delude ourselves when we think that way. I know it's old fashioned to quote from the Bible, but something you can find in Isaiah has always stuck in my mind since I was a child." Quietly I heard her recite:

> Yea, they shall not be planted; yea, they shall
> not be sown; yea, their stock shall not take
> root in the earth: and he shall also blow upon
> them, and they shall wither, and the whirl-
> wind shall take them away as stubble.

"Not cheerful stuff, Jamie, but so eloquently and so truly put. It was not our John's cup of tea. He always thought he'd been planted, rooted in his own good earth."

"Well, I suppose his thinking so is understandable. Years of hard toil on the land may well have created a sense of belonging which he found easy to accept. And I'm sure he never thought of himself as withering away."

"No, he certainly did not—and now the whirlwind has taken him up."

"I've wondered," I said, "of what he thought, if he did, after his stroke. He did so try to say something to us and to me in particular, but all I could get or guess at was Boy, his name for me, which I've always taken for granted as his offhand way of setting me apart. You've always called me Jamie. Why do you think he preferred Boy? Wasn't he sure of his paternal status?"

Mother sat still, her hands closed, and looking worriedly at me made no reply for several seconds. Then with a deep breath, almost a sigh, she said, "I must tell you something Jamie that John told me never to do. But he's gone, and I'm going to tell you now what I think we should have told you years ago. And oh Jamie! I hope you'll not condemn me for my silence, but, the truth is, you were not my own child."

"What do you mean?"

"You were," she said, her voice dropping, "an adopted baby."

If not a shock, mother's revelation bewildered me and left me full of questions, for I'd never doubted my parentage. As I regained some mental balance, I asked the

question that followed naturally from her confession:
"Why did the Old Man insist I should never be told?"

"Because he wanted others to believe you were his own offspring. He was a man to whom a child of his own making was his heart's desire. Not being able to achieve this end, he wanted his acquaintance never to doubt whose child you were. It was, I'm afraid, a false pride that drove him to insist upon your origin remaining a secret."

"And did you," I asked her, "treat me at all differently because I was not your own son?"

"No, Jamie, never! Ever since I first held you warm in my arms, you were my own baby—and what a lovely little fellow you were—missing nothing, just three days old. Oh, I was so pleased and John was, too. We had tried so often to have one of our own but no luck. And here you were ready-made to prosper our hopes."

"But where did you get me and why didn't our neighbours know about it?"

"Oh no one here could know; at that time we were living on a farm north of Kemptville. We did not buy this farm until you were nearly two years old. The neighbours here had no reason to question your parentage."

"And did you know who my parents were?"

"Never. When we got you in Toronto, we were told only that you were legally our child and that the natural mother could not be named. They did say, however, that she was a strong, healthy young woman."

Thinking of my own birth date, I told my mother that the woman must have given me up about January 5, 1919.

"Yes, mother said, "just three days after you were born. The Children's Aid lady said we were fortunate because for some time their babies for adoption had been much older than three days. She said, too, you had been breast fed. And Jamie I've often wondered how that mother felt when she took you from her breast—forever.

She must have suffered a terrible sadness."

"And how," I asked, "did you feed me once you had me home?"

"Oh, that was easy; you took to a bottle as easily and as naturally as if you'd been born to it."

"And what did the Old Man think of the product he got?"

"He was as delighted as I was. I think he thought of you as filling the gap left by Rob's death—as a son who would some day take over his farm. Rob, you know, was thirteen years younger than your father. John had taught him all he could about farming just as he did you."

"Well, I must admit I found a very good home, and I'm grateful."

"But can you forgive me Jamie—and John, too, for never telling you you were someone else's boy?"

Without really thinking, I protested, "I'm not and have never been someone else's boy—I'm your boy, the McKay Black's boy. My real mother did not want me, you did. As for not knowing, I'm sure it doesn't matter now."

This time it was mother who took my hands while she smiled through her tears saying only, "Oh, Jamie!" For a minute or so we sat saying nothing while my new identity confronted the established one—and mother's tears dried away.

It was she who spoke first: "It's time you and I went to bed, and tonight, at last, I'll go to sleep clear of the family secret. Leaning over to kiss me goodnight, she whispered, "and you are my own boy—and that's the end of it."

The next morning, after Geoffrey and the Logan boy had left the house and the dishes had been cleared away, mother made fresh coffee for us which we drank in the study where she said we needed to talk.

"We must be clear," she told me, "about the future of this farm. You and I for obvious reasons can't carry on here."

"So, what's to be done?" I inquired.

"There's really no alternative, we'll have to sell in the spring."

"And what chance is there of finding a buyer?"

"Rather good," she said. "Dutch people are buying farms in the Zorras. And ours is attractive to anyone familiar with land and buildings."

"And our cattle, horses, and farm machinery?" I queried. "Who's to look after all that when Geoffrey leaves?" Mother's response reminded me of how practical she, too, could be.

"That is a more urgent matter," she replied, "but I do remember a year ago, when Hugh Seaton's farm at Lakeside was sold, that all his stock and implements were auctioned off four or five months before the farm was advertised. We could do the same. Our herd of Holsteins is recognized by the Holstein Friesian Association to which your father belonged. It's one of the best in the township. As for Geoffrey I'm sure he'll stay with us for a time if I hire him by the day."

"Won't you miss the farm after all these years on it?" I asked.

"No, I don't think so, it's my John I'll miss. I've cried every night thinking of him when I reach out in bed and find he's not there. He was so much a part of me."

"Maybe a move to a new place will be cheering for you."

"Yes, a change will be good for me although I'm sure I'll always miss our Old Man. But what about yourself?"

"My four years away from home will make the transition easy. And, as my father often reminded me, I'm no longer physically able to farm."

"I think, Jamie, he was right on that score. You should find employment that makes more use of your mind than your body."

"Well then, let me begin by reminding you that we are to take the Chevy to Embro this afternoon for its winter tune-up. While I'm waiting for it you can visit friends."

"That's a good beginning Jamie, and I'll drive you down. But first I must get our noon meal. We can talk later."

We spent most of the afternoon in Embro returning in time to prepare supper for Geoffrey and Lorne. That done and the dishes cleared away, we sat late in the kitchen reviewing our decision to sell the farm deciding that the sale of the livestock should take place in November before the winter made travel difficult. That settled and talked out we went off to our beds where for an hour I lay thinking of mother and the Old Man, of a secret he made her keep, and of his farm she had now to sell. I thought, too, of a mother who had not wanted me and of one who was delighted to have me. Sleep blessedly put an end to thinking. I slept dreamlessly.

In the morning mother said that she, too, had had a good night's rest. "No tears at all, Jamie," she said smiling as we sat at breakfast.

From that day on we had much to do while we settled with Goody and Bustin's, sent out many letters of appreciation, saw a lawyer in Stratford about John's will, consulted with an auctioneer, and ended the lease on the Logan acres. Then we saw real estate people in Woodstock where my aunt was also looking for an apartment for my mother. The future was quietly drawing its curtain over the past.

Chapter 9

Mingled Yarn

November passed quickly. I was barely aware of the farm itself because Geoffrey was so familiar with its operation and worked so well with Lorne Logan. Shortly after the funeral, I was surprised to find the turnips were no longer in the field back the lane but stored away for the winter. Implements and wagons were under cover and by the middle of the month cattle off the pasture and in stanchions. Our farm was in good hands.

At the house mother and I were incredibly busy. I don't remember having the leisure to do much more than glance at the headings of *The Globe and Mail* that told of a nation-wide General Motors' strike in the States, of the Nuremberg trials, and the arrival of the Empress of Scotland in Halifax with over 4000 Canadian veterans on board. Making the arrangements for our livestock and implement sale took up all our spare time. It took place on November 27, just three days before a snow storm and freezing temperatures made travel on all the roads in the county risky.

But the sale went well, just old Caesar left with us by way of animal life. The day after, Geoffrey with his farewell cheque went away to better himself in a Stratford factory. The Logan boy went home saying he'd be available if we had any need for him. Tired and aching, mother was satisfied.

Because I had been on my feet a great deal before and after the sale, my stump had become very tender. I was so concerned lest blisters develop early in December I arranged for a quick trip to Toronto to have a Christie Street prosthetic artificer check the fit of the socket. He found, as I suspected, that it needed relining, and I had to spend a night in the hospital while that was being done.

While there I inquired at the main office for news of Fleda only to be told she had died the past week. The notice of death had been placed in *The Toronto Star*. The Nursing Sister in charge had little information except she'd heard the will left a large sum of money to the Christie Street Military Hospital to be used for amenities for veterans.

The news of her death saddened and bothered me because there was no one I could turn to for consolation. Like my phantom pains her death seemed unreal but hurting, a part of me in distress for someone I had wanted in vain. No use to expect understanding from the patients on the ward who were, I was sure, unaware of my feeling for Nursing Sister Fleda.

It was a relief the next day to get my leg back with new stump socks that cushioned the stump snugly in the relined socket. Once more I managed to find my way through Union Station to the train that took me to mother in Stratford. It was good to be with her in the house where in the evening over coffee in the familiar study we sat and talked of what was still to be accomplished.

"Now that we've got the stables emptied," she said, "you and I have to clear away the rubbish in this house."

"And what classifies as rubbish?" I asked.

"Look no farther," she answered, "than the corners of this room which is a memorial to a dear man, a very diligent pack rat, who never discarded a scrap of paper if he thought it might in his lifetime be needed. And, James McKay, it's your job; I want this room and desk cleaned out and, while you're at it, we must have a look to see what's stored away in the attic."

With nothing else to do and the memory of a tender stump, I welcomed a task at which I could sit and rely on crutches to get about. The work arrangement agreed to, mother suggested, as we sat under the yellow glow of two coal oil lamps was that the Old Man's memory called for a dram of what she termed his Islay mist. This time there were no tears, no talk of another mother, no talk of the sale—just mother recalling the first time I'd left home. It was the result of the Old Man acting on the advice of his Ag. Rep. who had convinced him that I should attend the Ontario Agricultural College once I'd completed Grade XII at S.C.V.I.

"I still remember the advantages," I told mother: "no need to spend a year in Grade XIII, lower fees than at Toronto or Western, an education geared to farming needs, and the possibility of earning the cost of my board and lodging by working as a stable hand."

"Oh, the Ag. Rep. was very persuasive," mother added. "The O.A.C. was the place to go if you intended to be a farmer like your father."

"And it was good advice," I told her. "My four years in college were lively. I liked it there for I was no longer a country boy as I had been in Stratford's Collegiate."

"You certainly changed," mother continued, as we breathed in Islay's comforting mist. "You became more independent—even found us a bit slow, didn't you?"

"You're right there. We were indoctrinated—maybe that's too strong a word—but we were led to believe in ourselves. And you conformed or else! Residence life was rather like the way a good regiment shapes you. As the professors were nearly all Aggies, they unwittingly contributed to the campus pattern of thought—we were all as our song put it 'for the O.A.C. by **heck**'."

"Anyway, Jamie, I don't think John made a mistake in sending you to the cow college. Its graduates are widely known, and I'm sure," she added, "that you'll find your place among them."

With this optimistic view of my future, we put Islay's mist back in its hiding place and went to bed where I dreamed of judging cattle under the direction of Scotty McLean who wouldn't know an Ayrshire from a Durham but was an able director of drama on the campus.

In the morning after breakfast, I set about examining stacks of old *Farmer's Advocates* and of farm reports flanking either side of the roll-top. The first problem was how to dispose of such a mass of paper. Furthermore, how was I on crutches or even with the leg on to mount the steep stairs to the attic? It was mother who had a solution:

"Let's get Lorne Logan to do the donkey work while you sort and make decisions. I'll telephone Jenny now and ask her if Lorne can come over right after lunch."

By one o'clock I had all the *Advocates* and reports labelled as trash and, when Lorne arrived, I told him to dig a pit well back of the house, get some used oil from the driveshed, and begin tearing the magazines apart so that they could be burned in the pit. Within an hour they were in flames.

Next he and mother went to the attic out of which came years of Eaton's Fall and Winter *Catalogues*, minutes of long-over township meetings, and a mass of publications from the Ministry of Agriculture which mice over the years had found an excellent source for nest-building needs. By late afternoon mother pronounced the attic clear and had Lorne busy sweeping the floor.

Meantime I began investigating the upper levels of the roll-top where I found a bundle of letters and notes from family as well as several years of Christmas cards received and carefully bound with elastic bands which broke as you took them off. As I had no idea who most of the correspondents were, I arranged the cards in tidy piles until mother came down when, with no hesitation, she condemned the lot to the flames. The day's end saw the cleanup completed save for a hive of drawers lower down in the roll-top. They were all locked. These we decided to leave until the next day when we could work in daylight.

In the morning a telephone call from Embro meant that mother had to go there because an old friend was very ill; before leaving she realized that she also had a Women's Institute meeting in the afternoon. "So you'll have to work alone," she said. "I'll find the keys for you to unlock the drawers—there are several keys, and you'll just have to try them to find those that fit. I'll be back at noon."

By nine o'clock I was alone in the study. In the top level of drawers I found recent invoices, tax receipts, fire insurance records, and a collection of old bank books; a current one showed a balance of $5270.66. With few exceptions I set all my findings aside for burning. Later in the morning, in a bottom drawer next to the one that harboured the whisky, I found a thin packet of old letters bearing a military stamp. They were on faded Salvation Army notepaper. None was longer than a page or two. They were bound with a bit of old ribbon; all had been addressed to my father and signed, "Your brother Rob." In the one on top, mailed from London, Ontario, April 12, 1915/Rob said he expected to leave Canada before long. The next was from West Sandling in Kent. He was well and would soon be on leave in London. Between this letter and the next was a postcard of the Tower of London which Rob had seen in January. Then there was nothing until May, 1916, when he spoke of being with his battalion in France. Two more brief letters in that year offered little information as they had been heavily inked by zealous censors. Another in 1917 told of his being wounded, hospitalized for three weeks, and returned to his unit in the trenches.

In March 1918, a letter spoke of his having been wounded again and more seriously. The next letter of April 3 was from a convalescent camp where he reported having had a "rousing good time" with—here the censor had inked out rank, name, and unit of someone who obviously had contributed to the good time. In the last paragraph Rob asked about mother: "Did she miss teaching?" He concluded by saying that "as soon as this bloody war is over, I'm coming home, and I may not be alone. Wish me luck, Your brother Rob."

The last letter was a brief note from one of Rob's battalion friends saying he was sorry to report that Rob had been killed on a raiding party near Valenciennes on October 1, 1918. Altogether this packet of letters was disappointing, as thin on news as the letters it held. But obviously the Old Man had treasured these last links with his only brother.

On her return from Embro, mother told me after lunch that I should keep Rob's letters. "They are not much, Jamie, but he was your uncle, and you should as his scroll has it, 'see to it that his name be not forgotten.' He was not, I know, your real uncle," she added, "anymore than I am your natural mother."

After a pause she exclaimed, "Rob was so handsome. He was my age, and he danced divinely. I would have said, 'yes, yes!' had he ever asked me to marry him, but he went off to war, and your father was left." She stopped, as startled as I was by her confession, and merely said, "you must remember Robert—as I hope you will me."

"Of course, I will," I told her. "You, and Robert, and the Old Man are my family and that, I'll never forget."

"And Jamie it was so thoughtful of you to look up Rob's grave and write to me with a picture of it. It meant so much to me that I had it framed to sit on our dresser beside his photograph. Was it much trouble to find his grave?"

"No, not at all. We were in a rest area at Kemmel on the Belgian border and were only fifty miles from Valenciennes. My colonel let me have a jeep and driver for the day's trip. The cemetery is the St. Roch on the north east side of Valenciennes. I thought it attractive with its old stone wall, lime tree, and box hedges."

"And the letter you sent," mother went on, "was one of the nicest I had from you. I've kept it in its envelope in my dresser drawer. You'll think me a silly old woman, but when I was alone in the room I often cried as I read it and looked at Rob's picture. John never knew how foolish I was."

"Not foolish," I countered. "Sentiment and tears reveal how human we are. God forbid that reason and commonsense sit always in judgement."

As she came to my side and patted my shoulder, she exclaimed, "Good gracious, look at the time! I'll have to leave or I'll be late for the Institute meeting. Her sudden leaving also served, I'm certain, as a coverup for tearful eyes as she hurriedly slipped into her coat and furs and out the door.

After she'd driven off, I set about cleaning all the empty drawers and pigeonholes in the roll-top of broken pens and pencils, of loose pennies and five-cent pieces, and the fine dust of years. After this bit of house cleaning and a fit of sneezing, I went on emptying the last two drawers almost at floor level. From one of these I retrieved a Great North Western telegraph message and a letter. The telegraph read:

"Deeply regret inform you 7891 Lieutenant Robert McKay infantry officially reported killed in action October 1. (Signed, Officer in Charge, Record Office, Ottawa)

The letter sent out two days later read:

Dear Mr. McKay, -

Will you kindly accept my sincere sympathy and condolence in the decease of that worthy citizen and heroic soldier, your brother, Lieutenant Robert McKay.

While one cannot too deeply mourn the loss of such a brave comrade, there is a consolation in knowing that he did his duty fearlessly and well, and gave his life for the cause of Liberty and the upbuilding of the Empire.

Again extending to you my heartfelt sympathy.

Faithfully,

Sam Hughes
Major General
Minister of Militia and Defence
for Canada

And that's all I found in that drawer. But beside it in an identical one, below some scraps of yellowed paper, I found a small booklet with the faded title "Officers Advance Book for the exclusive use of" followed by the name in block letters of LIEUT. McKAY, ROBERT. Within the front cover were a half-dozen stubs indicating withdrawals he had made in England, France, and Belgium. On April 3, 1918 he had withdrawn 1200 French francs, intended perhaps for the rousing week-end he had enjoyed while at the convalescent unit. Three or four un-used withdrawal forms tightly folded were still attached.

Half the back cover of the Advance Book was missing and the whole stained a dark brown. On the outside of the back cover, my uncle had kept addresses, but as the miss-ing part held the names, only the units to which these acquaintances belonged were left. Two of his friends belonged to the 58th Battalion, the third to #44 Casualty Clearing Station. It was the #44 which beguiled me as I thought it belonged to the casualty clearing unit Fleda had told me about during our dinner at the Royal York. Was it her name that belonged to this address? It could have been another person—a doctor or an orderly—but why in that case would my uncle have withdrawn so much money? A gambling debt?

For nearly an hour sitting on the floor on a pillow and leaning against one side of the roll-top, I tried to bring elusive evidence and conjecture to conclusion as I re-read the brittle letters and puzzled over the name that may have belonged to #44. If it were Fleda's, had she heard, I won-dered, of Rob's death? Tired and with no means of knowing, I was relieved to hear the kitchen door open and my mother's cheerful hello and have her help me up from the floor. Her meeting, she explained, had been brief as the president was ill at home.

"But tell me," she asked, as she removed her coat and beret, "how did the clean-up go? Surely you didn't sit here on your bottom all afternoon?"

"It was really interesting—and frustrating," I said, "for I found one of Uncle Robert's service booklets on which was a partial address."

"Whose address was it?" mother asked.

"Of that," I replied, "I cannot be at all certain for it might have been that of any one of a half-dozen men and women in an advanced casualty clearing station in France.

"But why does it interest you? What was the name?"

"That's the problem," I answered, "half the back page of the booklet is missing, only the addresses of three people remain."

"And why does one interest you more than the others?"

"It's one that belonged to someone at #44 Casualty Clearing, possibly a nurse whom I may have known at Christie Street Military Hospital."

"And what's her name?"

Embarrassed, I had to admit I did not know her surname.

"She was just," I said, "Nursing Sister Fleda to us, but she did tell me she'd been attached to a casualty clearing station in France in the first war, and unless I'm mistaken, she used the number 44."

"Then why don't you telephone the hospital, ask to speak to her, and find out if she knew a Robert McKay in France?"

"I wish I could," I replied, "but Sister Fleda died about a week after father did. I just found out about her death on my last visit to Christie Street."

"Well that's too bad," mother said. "May I see Rob's book?" I handed her the booklet and showed her the addresses.

"I don't remember" she said, "John ever showing this to me although I did see two or three letters once that Rob had written to him."

"Well," I told her, "they're all here."

"But these addresses certainly aren't much help without names," she went on, as she riffled through the stubs and opened out the unused withdrawal forms where she found, tucked in against the stapled binding, a small photograph of a woman's face. Showing it to me she asked, "who, I wonder, was this person?"

"Let me see," I said, as I took the faded picture and held it up to the light. It was the head of a nursing sister, for her veil told that much, and, although I could not be certain, it looked like a much younger Fleda. To mother I said, "it could be the lady we knew at Christie as Nursing Sister Fleda."

"I don't ever remember," mother said, "your mentioning the names of any of your nurses there. Was there something special about this one?"

"No," I replied cautiously. "I came to know her because there were two other MacKays on our ward, and she had to distinguish us. I told her to call me Boy as my father did. So on the ward I became just Boy to her."

"Was she a good nurse?"

"She was," I assured mother, "the best of the lot, very efficient and understanding of our needs. And so patient."

"And you liked her?"

"Oh yes, I looked forward to seeing her at my bedside whenever she was making her rounds."

"Odd that you never mentioned this nurse to us."

"Well," I replied disarmingly and not very truthfully, "it never occurred to me that you might be interested— and, of course, I did not know about Robert's letters or his Advance Book."

"And so where are we now?" mother asked. "What's nurse Fleda's picture doing in Rob's possession?"

"There may be a good reason," I told her as I picked out the letter of April 3, 1918 to show her the reference to a rousing good week-end.

"It does seem possible, doesn't it, that Rob and your nurse Fleda may have been together that week-end?"

"I think so," I said, "and I wonder how intimate they were. His letter certainly suggests as much."

"Well, of one thing you can be sure, your uncle would not have anticipated quiet walks and conversation over tea. If he was anything like your father, a girl needed to be both cunning and agile to keep her good name. Some men . . ." and here mother, embarrassed by her disclosure, said, "Oh dear, I am being a little shameless, am I not?"

"Perhaps not," I returned, "just predictive for Sister Fleda told me she had to return to Toronto before the war's end as she was not well."

"She might or might not have been pregnant, however; we're guessing only," mother cautioned.

"That's so," I agreed. "But assuming she did have a baby, why wouldn't she have got in touch with you? Surely Rob would have told her about his brother and about you whom he had known, even danced with?"

"Oh, I imagine he would have. But you must remember that having a child out of wedlock at that time was much more shameful than now—something that was usually hushed up. And a lady like Fleda, a complete stranger to us, would have been too ashamed to come to us and confess. To place the baby out for adoption would have been her only alternative. That's why it wasn't at all difficult then for John and me to find a baby to adopt."

"But," I interrupted, "is it just possible that the baby you got was Fleda's?"

About to reply, mother exclaimed, "Goodness me look at the time! It's after six, I must get us something to eat. We can talk later in the kitchen."

Left to myself in the study and worrying over the evidence of the past, I felt confused and embarrassed by the thought that my pin-up lady was being promoted to the status of a pin-up mother. This was not a progression I'd ever imagined. If true, my lineage and love affair provided a dead father with further evidence that his son was indeed a dim-witted bastard. Happily my self-debasement ended when mother called me to the supper table. Over a bowl of homemade soup, she asked me if my being adopted was going to make a difference to me.

"No, I'm sure it won't," I answered, "because I can think only of you and father as my parents. But I admit it is a bit unhinging to accept Sister Fleda as my mother."

"But here," mother objected, "your putting motherhood on Fleda is supposition only. And further, to assume that the baby we got had to be hers is equally unlikely. Don't you agree?"

"Yes I have to and can only hope it's so."

"Why do you hope it's so? What's troubling about Fleda being your natural mother?"

"Nothing," I said evasively. "The possibility just astonishes me. And yet if she were my mother, she may have guessed as much. Rob must have given her his name and told her of his brother who would be shown as my next-of-kin on my medical chart at Christie Street where she'd see the date of my birth. She was very interested in my appearance, blue eyed, fair-haired, not at all a McKay Black. Even so she could not possibly be certain that it was her baby that you and father got in Toronto."

"Oh, I think we do lack convincing evidence for your origin," mother asserted, "and we may well be wronging your Fleda. At the same time I'm pleased you may have had such a mother and father. No cause for shame. Quite acceptable—just so long as there's no discounting of me!"

"No fear of that," I replied. "You're not for sale in my shop."

"Well, that's kind of you Jamie and heart easing. Thank you. And now we'd better put things away and wash up."

The kitchen tidy and sticks of split maple put in the McClary, we sat in the warmth while evening brought its shadows comfortingly around the house. I listened as my mother spoke quietly words which stilled the questioning of the past.

"As we can never be certain about the role your Uncle Robert and Nursing Sister Fleda played in your creation or that the child we adopted was theirs, I suggest we should, as the Old Man would say, use our commonsense and leave Rob and Fleda in that eternal silence that some day must shroud us all . . . do I have your consent?"

"Yes," I said, "you and I meantime have our ends to shape, our own gardens to plant and tend. What we cannot know should, as you suggest, be dignified by silence."

"I'm afraid, however, that gardening," mother warned me, "must be accepted only as a figure of speech. Arthritic fingers and a peg leg are ill-suited to hoeing and weeding, wouldn't you agree?"

"Objection heard and accepted," I answered. "But when I visit you let's not forget the joys of other gardens we've known when we sit at ease on your balcony taking tea and biscuits warm from the oven of your new electric stove."

"Now I like that idea," mother replied, "and I hope you'll come often to see me."

"Of course, I will. You and I must remain the best of friends as long as we walk together here below."

"Nothing could please me more. And now may I suggest we walk off to our beds where who knows what gardens we'll dream about tonight."

Later, nursing some phantom pain and watching an indifferent white moon slip beyond my window's frame, I thought for a time of the Old Man and his brother Rob —the McKay Blacks—and of mother and me. What lay behind in the past was a marbled inheritance of mishap and blessing. What lay ahead was a blank page of uncertain length, a page that would always, on close inspection, reveal the watermark of an elusive lady as silent now as this moving moon.

Acknowledgments

I owe much to the kindness of Lt. Col. R.S. Chamberlain M.C., "Bomber," and to Mr. Corrie Kool for telling me about Holwierde in the Netherlands during the night of April 23/24, 1945.

For information about the Perth Regiment, I have consulted Stafford Johnston, *The Fighting Perths*; and Stanley Scislowski, *Not All of Us Were Brave*.